D1760938

0045297193

ENGLAND'S MISTRESS

Elizabeth Tudor has survived uncertainty and danger to ascend the throne. Now Europe waits to see whom she will choose as her husband from her many suitors. Only Elizabeth herself knows that she is wedded to England — an England under threat from Spain. But, most of all, the country is menaced by a queen from across the border who regards the Tudor throne as rightfully hers. The stage is being set for a duel to the death between Elizabeth and the Queen of Scots.

MAUREEN PETERS

ENGLAND'S MISTRESS

Complete and Unabridged

LINFORD
Leicester

First published in Great Britain in 1991 by
Robert Hale Limited
London

First Linford Edition
published 1998
by arrangement with
Robert Hale Limited
London

British Library CIP Data

Peters, Maureen, *1935* –
    England's mistress.—Large print ed.—
    Linford romance library
    1. Love stories
    2. Large type books
    I. Title
    823.9'14 [F]

    ISBN 0–7089–5247–X

Published by
F. A. Thorpe (Publishing) Ltd.
Anstey, Leicestershire

Set by Words & Graphics Ltd.
Anstey, Leicestershire
Printed and bound in Great Britain by
T. J. International Ltd., Padstow, Cornwall

This book is printed on acid-free paper

1

IN the Presence Chamber the conversation was muted and discreet. One never knew when Cecil, mild-eyed and soft-footed, might not come creeping or some lackey of Milord Leicester be all ears in a forgotten corner. Not to mention the Queen herself. Elizabeth had sharp ears and sharper eyes, and. could winkle out gossip at fifty paces.

She sat now in this the tenth year of her reign on the carved and canopied throne, her curled red-gold head inclined to the French Ambassador, Fenelon La Motte. Her long, exquisite fingers were adorned with rings and glowed and throbbed in the lights from the lanterns that were suspended from wrought iron poles set at angles in the walls. She haloed in light, an effect heightened by the coronet of gold set with pearls and moonstones on her hair and the stiffly starched collar of gold lace that rose up behind her head. Her dress of apricot satin was sewn with tiny brilliants that flashed and sparkled as she turned her slender figure to lean closer to the elegant figure of La Motte.

"Is it my fault," she was asking, "if four Spanish trading ships are chased by Channel pirates into my ports and there seek refuge?"

"It depends on who does the chasing, Your Grace," the ambassador said slyly.

"Perhaps it was French pirates."

"Who would in that case have chased the vessels into French ports, surely?"

"Not if the tides were running against them."

"I have noticed," he said, "that the tides of the Channel often run in England's favour."

"Who can argue against the will of God?" She gave him a sweetly innocent smile, and then frowned. "One can, however, argue against the will of Spain. My brother in law is too apt to claim every lost vessel as his own property. As far as I can ascertain there is some doubt as to whether the said ships come within his jurisdiction since they are manned by men of the Netherlands who claim independence."

"Your Grace would support rebels?"

Her finely plucked brows arched over the long, sea-coloured eyes that seemed to change shade according to her mood. "Lord forfend! Never would I support rebels against their annointed monarch," she said.

"My own king will be happy to hear that," La Motte said. "The Huguenots still cause him great anguish."

"Surely they ask only for the freedom to worship God as they believe."

"Heresy is still a crime," he said.

"And the Catholic heretic is too often the Protestant martyr." She sighed briefly. "I tell you frankly, Mr Ambassador, that though I have reaffirmed the Protestant faith here in this land I wink my eye on my many subjects who still cling to the Roman rite. Who am I to make windows into men's souls?"

"Perhaps Your Grace's views are influenced by your own personal experiences?" he said.

"Faith, but it would be strange if they were not," she agreed. "My father broke from Rome in order to marry my mother and then my sister threw out all the reforms of my brother's reign and lit the fires of Smithfield to encourage people to obey. Too many have died for their faith on both sides. I'll not add to the number of martyrs."

"So you will not return the Spanish ships?"

"Why, let Philip come and take them," she said, smiling. "He offered me marriage after my poor sister died, her heart broken by his neglect. Let him come visit me if he wishes."

"Touching the matter of Your Grace's marriage — " He paused as her eyes brightened. Talk of marriage always revitalised her, bringing a sparkle to her countenance and a liveliness to her voice.

"I am inclined to remain a spinster," she said.

"And cheat England of heirs? That would be a crime, Majesty."

"Oh, there are plenty who would argue that already I have too many heirs," she said lightly. "There's my cousin of Scots who will have it that she is already rightful queen of this realm, and her puling son, and the sisters of Milady Jane who are both practically half-witted if you want my frank opinion, and the brother of the late Darnley and — but I will not name any heir. Why should I? Though I'd choose to stay unwed I am aware that women have a duty to bear children, and even a queen is not exempt."

"My master of France offered for your hand."

"An offer I am considering," she said loftily.

"Madam, there must be a time limit

on consideration," La Motte protested. "It is now nearly five years since the offer was made."

"My main objection was that King Charles was too young."

"He has aged five years since then."

"And so have I," she said sadly. "The gap between us has not lessened."

"Your Grace was not waiting for it to do so, I venture to assert. In actual years he will always be younger, though he is now fully mature in all ways."

"But still younger than I," Elizabeth said. "And much ruled by his lady mother, or so the report runs. Catherine de Medici will like better a daughter-in-law whom she can mould to her wishes."

"Queen Catherine would be delighted to welcome you into France," La Motte protested.

"But how could I stay there when I have a country of my own to rule? And the King of France could scarcely spend all his time in England attendant upon my whims. There would be long

6

periods of separation which is not conducive to marital bliss. I have my late sister's sad example."

"A union between France and England would act as a counterweight to Spain's territorial ambitions."

"That," she agreed, "would be an advantage to us both. But your king is still younger than I."

"Were you to meet him you would imagine him to be older," La Motte said promptly, "as he would think you younger than your years were he to meet you. I speak of looks, not of quality of mind."

"And what of Elisabeth of Austria?" the queen asked.

"I beg Your Grace's pardon?" La Motte had flushed.

Elizabeth furled her jewelled fan and ran its edge down his bearded cheek.

"Come, my friend," she purred. "All this nonsense about a marriage between the King of France and myself when I know full well that Charles is practically betrothed to the Emperor's girl."

"Walsingham, I suppose?" La Motte looked defeated.

"His news is always accurate," Elizabeth said. "So is Charles seeking to wed both of us at once?"

"Were you to change your mind and accept we would hear no more of Elisabeth of Austria."

"It is not a question of changing my mind but of coming to a decision," she said, growing faintly irritated. "Your master is in a great hurry to be wed. I'll not be rushed into any bridal yoke."

"Then he will offer for the Emperor's daughter which would be a personal grief to me," the ambassador said, "for I can think of none more suited to rule both France and England than yourself."

"How wise was Queen Catherine to appoint you as ambassador!" Elizabeth chuckled. "You will have to make do with the other Elisabeth, I fear. I'll not be a rival for a monarch still ruled by the Queen Mother, greatly as I revere her name. So what other candidate have you lingering in the shadows?"

"My master has a brother."

"Your master has two brothers. Which one has he in mind as a replacement for himself?"

"His younger brother is noted for his beauty," La Motte said.

"Anjou?" Elizabeth snapped open her fan and gave an angry little laugh. "Anjou is, if my memory doesn't deceive me, even younger than his elder brother, or are you about to tell me there was a muddle at birth?"

"I would not insult your intelligence so," La Motte assured her. "However the Duke of Anjou is even more mature for his age than the king is for his, and exceedingly handsome. A match between you would also halt the pretensions of Spain."

"True." Elizabeth was silent, pensive. Sooner or later she would have to take a husband, she supposed. Her right to rule England was constantly attacked by the Papists who wanted to see Mary Stuart upon the throne. With a husband she could sleep more securely — but it had to be the right husband. So far she had loved only two men. Sir Thomas Seymour had been her first love, married to her widowed stepmother, Catherine Parr, but waking in her own young heart a romantic passion that had been nipped short cruelly when she had learned of his execution as traitor. Even now, when she half closed her eyes, she could see his arrogant black head and hear his loud laughter echoing through the garden of Chelsea Manor.

The second she loved still and always would. They were born on the same hour on the same day in the same year. Their lives had been twined together ever since as children they had played together. It was a thousand pities that Leicester's wife had died in such suspicious circumstances. Had she married him after Amy Robsart had been discovered lying with a broken neck at the foot of the staircase the scandal might have toppled her from the throne. A parallel scandal had actually toppled the Queen of Scots for Mary Stuart had married the Earl of Bothwell who was certainly implicated in the murder of her husband, Darnley.

As if he read the tenor of her thoughts La Motte said, "Speaking of the Queen of Scots — "

"Which we were not," Elizabeth said, controlling a start.

"My master frets that she has been moved from Bolton Castle to Tutbury. He wonders at the reason for it."

"The air is more healthful at Tutbury," Elizabeth said.

"It is not so near the border either."

"So her rebellious subjects cannot do her any mischief while she is my guest," Elizabeth said.

"If you permitted her to travel on to France — "

"Oh, I could not in conscience give her safe conduct until the question of guilt or innocence in the matter of the Lord Darnley's murder is cleared up."

"Then she is prisoner."

"My honoured guest. One day I hope we will meet and talk as two cousins," Elizabeth said. "It would be very foolish of me to allow her to travel on to a country where so many regard her as the rightful queen of this realm, don't you think?"

"If Your Majesty agrees to marriage with Anjou that problem will loom less large," La Motte said.

"As to that we shall see. Is he truly handsome? Portraits can lie."

"He is very handsome, but if you invite him to visit you then you may judge for yourself."

"You must give me time to think about it. My mind was almost set upon wedding King Charles, and now I must turn it to his brother, it seems. You will excuse me now, Mr Ambassador? I see my courtiers whispering that I keep you overlong. You would not have scandal bracket our names?"

"Madam, I would count it as a great honour," he said fervently, "save that I fear nobody would ever believe that a lady like you would even look twice at a humble diplomat."

"Go to!" She brushed his cheek with the edge of her fan again and rose, her satin skirts belling about her.

As she rose so the whispered conversations were stilled, eyes followed her progress across the floor. When she paused at a group the gentlemen bowed; the ladies dipped into deep curtsies. When she made a jest they laughed; when she frowned their own faces mirrored it. It had been thus with her father, great Harry the Eighth as he bestrode his Court like a Colossus. In the end his presence had inspired fear. For herself she craved loving respect mingled with awe. So far she judged herself successful in obtaining it.

"Is the gossip spicy in the Court of France?" Robert Dudley, Earl of Leicester broke custom by addressing her first. Robin, she thought tolerantly, was of the opinion that etiquette was for others to follow.

"Nothing I did not suspect already.

Walk with me, Rob."

She took his arm and moved towards a side door that opened into one of the pleasance bowers that surrounded the palace of Greenwich. The weather was still mild despite the month of November, and a few fading roses clung yet to the spiked bushes beyond the rosemary borders.

"Only smell the perfumes of the evening," she said softly. "It soothes the soul."

"Does Your Grace feel the need of soothing?" he enquired.

"I have problems," she admitted. "England has problems, Robin."

"And you are England," he said, not flattering, but stating a fact with simplicity.

"I am also a woman. With you I am a woman." She took his arm, looking up into his face, made hawk-like by the pale moon that rayed down through the bare branches of the apple trees.

"Not completely," he said. "Not to

14

the farthest limits, my Bess. When will that be?"

"You ask too much," she said, withdrawing her hand abruptly. "I have warned you before not to press me."

"No doubt you are saving yourself for Anjou," he said.

"So you too have heard how the wind blows in the Court of France?" Forgetting her pique she took his arm again, strolling on. "King Charles grows weary of my tardiness and will take the daughter of the Emperor Maximillian, and I am offered Anjou. What think you?"

"That you are unlikely to lap the bounds with that simpering powder-puff."

"Rumour speaks true then?" She chuckled softly. "Yet it is possible for a man to turn and then to turn again, don't you think? If he remained with me long enough to sire an heir I would make no complaint. It would still ensure a bulwark against Spain and a check to those who would see

15

my cousin of Scots on my throne."

"Of which there are more than Your Grace is aware," Leicester said.

"Meaning?"

They had reached the end of an avenue and she swung round, loosing her hold, her voice sharp.

"Milord of Norfolk is writing letters to your royal guest, hinting broadly that if she were to take a fourth husband then himself need not be despised."

"Norfolk and Mary of Scots? Over my dead body!"

"Yes, Madam," he said dryly.

"Norfolk has ideas above his station even if he is premier duke. The letters are proved?"

"So Walsingham tells me. There is no treason in the penning of a letter."

"That depends on the contents. So Norfolk sees himself as the next husband of Mary Stuart?" She was silent a space, gnawing her underlip.

"Neither is it treason to wed," Leicester said mildly.

"His only reason for casting his eyes

in that direction," Elizabeth said, "is for gain. What gain could there be in his espousing a disgraced and deposed queen unless he meant to set her on another throne?"

"Then you yourself must wed and bear a son," he told her frankly.

"You, I suppose?"

"As well myself as any powder-puff prince."

"But you cannot stand between me and the threat of Spain."

"Is marriage for love out of fashion?" He caught her to him, looking down into her moon-glinted face. It was a delicate face, the cheekbones high, the brow lofty under the tightly curled hair. In old age it would be a scimitar of a face with nose hooked and lips pulled tight, but now in her high summer it was proud and comely. Her long eyes slanted at him, promising more than she had ever consented to perform; her white skin smelled of lavender.

"They would remember how your wife met her end," she reminded him.

"For God's sake, Bess, must you fling poor, dead Amy in my teeth every time I ask you to wed me?" he exclaimed. "The Board of Enquiry cleared me of all suspicion in the affair. Amy fell from the top of the staircase at Cumnor Hall. I did not push her."

But when the body was found someone had modestly straightened her skirt. That fact was engraved on her mind.

"And if there is scandal," he was continuing, "why, you are the crowned and anointed queen. You may ignore gossip."

A breeze blew gently through the trees, stirring the grasses, bending the leafless boughs. There had been other queens who had flouted convention. Her own mother had ignored King Harry's frowns and flirted with her intimate circle, hiding her heartache at her failure to give him a son under constant feverish gaiety. She had been less than three when her mother had been executed. Yet she had an abiding memory of that high, wild laughter echoing across the small, enclosed world of her childhood. She had no picture in her mind of her mother's face beyond the portrait of her she had seen. The portrait was stiff and lifeless and her mother had sparkled with life, black eyes inviting conversation, black hair tossing beneath the heart shaped caps of silk and velvet that she had favoured. But when Elizabeth tried to conjure up that face she could see only a headless trunk, blood spurting from the neck, the black hair splashed with the gore as it rolled away into the straw. Five men had died with her mother, accused of carnal knowledge of their queen, and one of them her own brother. Yet all the proof had rested merely in lightsome conversation, a dance too closely danced, a look flung in the wrong direction.

"I cannot allow my personal affections to weigh against the good of the realm," she said.

"So you will take Anjou and care

nothing for my jealousy?"

"I will take Anjou," she agreed, "but you need never be jealous of him — or any man. This will be a marriage of state, Robin, undertaken purely to stop the pretensions of Spain and provide the realm with an heir. My heart is not involved, I assure you."

At her own words a pang of self-pity swept over her. Other more fortunate women might wed where their hearts dictated, but she must always set her own desires in accord with the good of the land. The problem was that she was not sure of her own heart's yearnings. She had loved Robert Dudley ever since the first, wild passion for Tom Seymour had ended in his death on the scaffold. To have him at her side as her close companion and to accept his compliments and caresses satisfied the hungry child within her but when he would have claimed more the woman withdrew back, the image of a neck spurting blood rising in her mind. There were times when the execution of her mother whose features stayed in shadow became confused with another death. Her tiny stepmother, Katheryn Howard, whom King Harry had named his rose without a thorn had never lived long enough to bloom. There had been a day when the eight-year-old Elizabeth had whirled round in a step of Queen Kat's devising, only to hear the music cease as her uncle of Norfolk, father to the present duke, said,

"It is no more the time to dance."

And Katheryn too had bowed her head upon the block.

"You are shivering," Leicester said in concern.

"Orchards are cold places in November," she answered, and breaking from him, ran back up the narrow avenue. He caught up with her, swinging her back into his arms.

"One kiss to warm my bones?" He kissed her without waiting for her answer, his lips clinging to her own half-open, eager mouth.

"Faith, you talk as if you were

already old," she chided, breaking free at last. "You are five and thirty, my Rob, and in your prime. Perhaps it is you who should be courting the Queen of Scots?"

"Thank you, but I'll not venture within that siren embrace," he said. "I do not forget how the Lord Darnley died, strangled in the wreckage of his lodgings, while his widow eloped with that savage lord most suspected of the murder."

"Have you warned Norfolk of his folly in writing to that queen?" she asked abruptly.

"Both Cecil and I warned him."

"Well, it is unusual to find you and Cecil in accord about anything," she grinned.

"Each of us distrusts the ambitions of the other but in our loyalty to you we are united."

"What did my cousin of Norfolk say?"

"That he would think very hard before he laid his head upon the same pillow as that of a lady so deeply suspicioned."

"Let us hope he takes his own advice." She turned and went back into the sheltering wings of the palace.

She had been born in this palace, in the Chamber decorated with tapestries depicting the birth of the Virgin. Her mother, disappointed at her sex, had made a gallant pun, crying,

"See, my liege, in the chamber of the Virgin I too bring forth a virgin." She would not have guessed in her wildest dreams that thirty five years later that babe would still be a virgin.

"Complete penetration is not impossible," her physician had confided to her, "though it might be painful unless the hymen has previously been stretched. But there is no serious impediment to Your Grace's marrying and bearing children."

No impediment save the bloodstained images crowding into her mind when a man reached for the core of her femaleness. No impediment save the knowledge that when you yielded entirely to any man then death pounced, wearing her father's face.

The Court was at Greenwich to avoid the plague that had visited London for too long a time, leaving many families bereaved. The royal family too had been bereaved, the Queen's cousin, Lady Knollys, dying during the epidemic. Elizabeth had wept over her cousin's death. The Knollys clan were children and grandchildren to her aunt, Mary Boleyn, who had borne King Harry a son before the king's small grey eyes had lighted on her more fascinating sister. At Greenwich the river ran tranquil to the sea and the few bracing days of wind and snow blew ill health away. She rose early and walked briskly in the gardens that ran down to the shore, taking a malicious pleasure in outstripping her less energetic ladies who panted after her, wishing they could toast their feet in front of a blazing fire.

"Where they will grow fatter having

gorged themselves too much at table," Kat Ashley said.

Her former governess was elderly now — one might say old had not Kat's own spryness made the word ridiculous. It was impossible to envisage life without Kat who had been part of her life ever since she could remember. Kat was a gossip and occasionally took a little more wine than she could discreetly hold, but when Kat died there would be nobody left to scold and speak her mind as she was now doing.

"Anjou indeed. I never thought the day would come when I saw you considering the suit of a popinjay."

"His reputation may have been exaggerated."

"He hasn't fathered any bastards," Kat said triumphantly. "That proves his tastes are peculiar."

"It proves nothing of the kind," Elizabeth said, amused, "and my marriage cannot possibly be based purely on personal considerations. I must think of the good of the realm."

"A pity others are not so mindful of their duty," Kat said sourly. "You jest about those who would write love letters to the Queen of Scots when they have never laid eyes on her, but to my mind that's plain treason."

"My cousin of Norfolk has assured Cecil that he recognizes the folly of such a course."

"Does he so?" Kat pursed her lips. "Then why is the Queen of Scots still writing to him, calling him her 'sweet Norfolk' and declaring she longs to meet him? I had it from Mr Walsingham yesterday."

"Since when does my minister make his reports to my servant?" Elizabeth demanded.

"Since you go scrambling through hedgerows with Milord Leicester and leave your minister to kick his heels in the hall."

"So he gave you some messages which you wait a full day before you pass on to me. Why?"

"I was never in a hurry to give bad

news," Kat said. "Your life should be led in sunlight, my sweeting."

"So should all lives. What news?"

"Rumours of disaffection in the north."

"There have been rumours of disaffection in the north since my great grandsire sat upon the throne," Elizabeth said impatiently. "They never come to much."

"When they have a Catholic queen set down in their midst and a duke eager to wed her with promised help from Spain it might yet come to something."

"Is rebellion planned then?"

Her face had sobered. She jerked her head from the brush that Kat was wielding and stared at the other.

"So Mr Secretary thinks, though as yet final proof is lacking."

"If the north rises," Elizabeth said slowly, "with the intention of putting the Queen of Scots in my place then Spain may well send help. Oh, why did that wretched woman have to flee from her subjects into my territory?"

"She expected Your Grace to aid her," Kat said.

"I cannot help her without putting my own position in jeopardy," Elizabeth said angrily.

"And you cannot hand her over to the Scottish rebels because she is an anointed queen and your near kin," Kat added. "You're in a coil, my lovesome."

"I will take Anjou as husband," Elizabeth said, heaving a small, unconscious sigh. "If I agree to that then France will cease to press for Mary's claims. Catherine de Valois has no real sympathy for her. It will suit her better to set her precious son upon the English throne, even if that means she has to take me as a daughter-in-law. And Philip of Spain will prudently think twice before he moves against an Anglo-French alliance."

That the Duke of Anjou was younger than herself, a painted doll of a young man could not be allowed to matter. Her people would see only the advantages of the union. She would keep the bridegroom at her side long enough to provide her with an heir of her own body and then pack him back to his boyfriends and his formidable mother.

"Let's to supper." She allowed Kat to twitch the last curl into place and rose; her silvery skirts falling into beams of moonlight about her.

"You look beautiful today," Kat said fondly.

"And much good may it do me," her mistress said lightly. "To please Anjou it would be better if I were breeched, I daresay. Come."

Even when the supper was a private affair in one of the smaller chambers the trumpets still sounded, the heads and knees were still bowed. Always, everywhere she was Queen and must remind even those closest to her of that fact.

"My dear cousin of Norfolk." She paused by him, watching him straighten from his bow. He was a thin, fair man, very different from his darkly saturnine father. Her uncle of Norfolk had been related to her mother directly through the marriage of his youngest sister to a Bullen. He had risen high in royal favour in her father's time, and had helped to push two of his nieces to the throne only to sink into disfavour after their disgraced ends. Yet he had out-lived Great Harry's reign, and bred this gentle seeming son who flushed now, biting his lip.

"Your Grace." He looked guilty even before he was accused, Elizabeth thought scornfully. Was he really so stupid as to continue writing love letters to Mary Stuart after she had had him warned?

"We don't have the delights of your company often enough," she said. "Perhaps your correspondence keeps you busy?"

"No, indeed." His mouth had rounded in dismay.

"Have a care to the pillow you

sleep on, my dear cousin," she said
softly, and leaning, pinched his cheek
between her sharp nails hard enough
to draw a few drops of blood from the
pale flesh.

2

"**P**ERHAPS I will take the Archduke Charles after all," Elizabeth said thoughtfully.

"It is three years since he offered," Cecil objected.

"I told him then that I needed time in which to consider his proposal," she retorted. "Now it seems to me that it might be more advantageous for me to take the archduke than the French prince. It would be a set-down for both Spain and France, and the archduke does not have Catherine de Valois as a mother, which predisposes me mightily in his favour."

"Your Grace wishes me to open the negotiations again?"

"I will send young Cobham to talk with the archduke privately," she decided. "If he still desires the match then more experienced diplomats can step in to clinch the bargain."

"And Anjou?" Her chief minister glanced at her.

"For the now let Anjou rest." She leaned back in her chair, regarding him from under nervously frowning brows. In the summer she was often nervous, disliking the intense heat that brought with it fresh outbreaks of plague. In the hot season old wrongs often festered and broke out into riot.

"Your Grace is anxious." It wasn't a question. Cecil knew his royal mistress's moods as well as he knew his own.

"I have heard the mutterings from the north," she said. "They grow into shouts and the shouts all cry the same theme. England for the Pope and Mary Stuart for Queen."

"My agents are watching closely," he assured her.

"Will they go on watching until the Catholics move south?" she asked dryly. "God's Blood, Cecil, we are all watching. It is proof of planned treasons I need, not reports on what may be going on."

"Milord Norfolk is still writing love letters," Cecil told her.

"Arrest him."

"It is not treason to write letters to a lady."

"When the lady has her eyes fixed upon my throne and when the letter writer is a convinced Catholic then it begins to look like disloyalty at the least. Arrest Norfolk — on suspicion of plotting. He can do no harm shut up under house arrest."

"As Your Grace pleases." Cecil looked unhappy.

"So what ails my fox?" The queen looked at him sharply.

"In your father's time men were sent to the Tower with no excuse save that their continued freedom embarrassed him. I hoped those days were dead."

"Amen," she answered promptly. "I have reigned so far with mercy as well as justice, but if there are mice nibbling at the foundations of your house will you not set traps? When my cousin of Norfolk pens his letters of devotion to Mary of Scots he nibbles at the foundations of my kingdom. I mean him no harm, Cecil. A good fright may be the making of him."

"Or precipitate that we most wish to avoid," he said sombrely.

"With Norfolk confined to his own estate the others will hesitate," she said confidently. "I may be betrothed to the Archduke Charles by Yuletide."

"Have you received word from the Queen of Scots?"

"A letter two days since, full of impertinences. She begins by reminding me that she fled to me seeking help against her rebellious lords and has instead been detained against her will in what she terms evil case. She informs me that she had no evil intent against me, and wishes to be my good sister. And she informs me that many in the north pity her case and would help her."

"She is remarkably straightforward," Cecil marvelled.

"She threatens me in my own kingdom," Elizabeth frowned, "I answered her, reminding her in my turn that she still is suspected of complicity in the death of her husband, that she has never renounced her claim to the throne of England and that, if she does not heed my words, she may find some of her supporters the shorter by a head — for so they would have been in my father's time. I spoke her plain."

"She is reckless," he allowed.

"So is Norfolk if he thinks still of matching himself with her against my wishes. Can you picture with calm a new Papist party led by Mary Stuart and Norfolk?"

"It will not come to that," he assured her. "Norfolk is a dreamer who sees Mary Stuart as a princess in need of a champion, that's all."

"And I am to be denied champions, I suppose? I too have been in durance but never have I acted as stupidly as she does."

But that was not so. There had been a time when she too had taken risks, stealing out for a boat ride with Tom Seymour while Kat Ashley wrung her hands in vain, sending messages to Robin when both were confined in the Tower and under threat of death. She had not always been completely cautious. In the years since she had learned to dissemble, to keep her intentions hidden even from the few she trusted, to watch and listen and wait. She had spent her whole life waiting. She would not now risk losing what patience had brought her.

The long hot summer wore on. At least at the palace of Greenwich there was less risk of plague with all those who came and went carefully questioned as to where they had been and how they felt, with huge bunches of herbs strung across the doorways of every chamber, and the salt air from the sea blowing through the gardens to expel evil humours.

Norfolk was arrested and confined to

his house where Elizabeth trusted he would spend a few months contemplating the folly of wooing dangerous queens.

With the autumn young Cobham returned crestfallen from his visit to the archduke, bearing a gift of a silver cup and a letter which Elizabeth read with mounting indignation.

"The Archduke Charles begs my pardon but, believing that I was no longer interested in making a match with him he has entered into an engagement with the princess of Portugal. He feels that he cannot in conscience withdraw now from his promise to her and begs to remain my good brother. How say you to that, Master Walsingham." She threw the letter down on the Council table and glared at her minister.

"The archduke has taken second best," he said.

"Don't try to soften me with flatteries," she said crossly. "The princess of Portugal may have two heads for all I care. How is it that I was not informed that he was already betrothed before I sent Master Cobham to make a fool of himself on my behalf?"

"Your Grace, I was not aware of it," he hastened to say. "You have not spoken of any betrothal with the archduke for three years."

"I told Cecil."

"And I would have informed Master Walsingham," her chief minister said promptly, "had not the present circumstances of plague rendered all travel within the realm subject to the most vexatious delays."

"Walsingham ought to have known what was afoot without having to wait for letters from Cecil," Elizabeth said unreasonably. "I employ you to find out how matters stand in other Courts. I do not expect you to sit at home waiting for the mail messenger to arrive."

"I stand corrected," Walsingham said stiffly, his long face drawn into frowning sulkiness.

"If I may speak," Cecil said, "I

would place the blame at my door for I ought to have ensured that Master Walsingham was kept fully informed but the ever constant fear that the plague might strike our beloved ruler made me tardier than I should have been in the sending of a message."

"Well, there is no great harm done." Elizabeth relented and shot her flashing smile about the table. "This princess of Portugal is the archduke's own niece, is she not? I would think twice before I wed a man willing to marry his own niece. It goes close to incest in my view."

"Your Grace is as usual neat in your judgement," Leicester said.

"And I did keep the poor man waiting overlong for an answer to his proposal. Both he and the King of France grew weary and took other brides. Don't you think I ought to send some definite answer to the suitor who remains?"

She looked archly round the semicircle of faces, but instead of the lively discussion on the subject of her marriage that she envisaged Walsingham said gravely,

"In the matter of the archduke I was at fault, but I have not been laggard in every direction. My information from the north is worrisome."

"What information?"

"The Catholics of Yorkshire and Lancashire are massing under a banner which depicts the five wounds of Christ," he told her.

"Another pilgrimage of Grace?" She sat up, her eyes narrowing. "Surely they are not so dull that they cannot distinguish between my late father and myself. Though like him I style myself truly as Head of the Church I have never made minute enquiry into the opinions of all my subjects on the matter. Provided the Catholics pay their recusancy fines and do not draw others into their net I am well content to leave sleeping dogs to snore."

"There are many good and loyal Catholics who applaud Your Grace's clemency," Cecil told her, "but there are still those who want to turn back the clocks to the days when King Harry was wed to the Spanish Catherine and paid tribute to the Pope."

"If your own legitimacy is questioned," Walsingham said, "then the queen is your cousin of Scotland."

"After all these years who dares now to question my legitimate rights barring a few fanatics?" she demanded.

"Milord of Norfolk for one," Walsingham told her.

"Norfolk is under house arrest," she said sharply.

"But not wasting his time in contemplating past errors," he said.

"Speak plain." She rapped the table with the handle of her ivory fan, looking as if she regretted that his knuckles were not nearer.

"To speak plain then, Your Grace, Milord Norfolk has sent word to the Queen of Scots that as a loyal Catholic he supports her claim to the throne of England and offers her his hand in marriage as soon as Your Majesty is removed from that eminence."

"Who leads the rebels? Norfolk cannot do so in person," she said.

"The Earls of Northumberland and Westmoreland," Walsingham said.

"Northumberland would seek to place a monkey on the throne provided it curtsied to the Pope, and Westmoreland is wedded to Norfolk's sister though Jane Howard is a devout Protestant lady," Elizabeth said.

"And in the north they wield great influence. Their countrymen will follow them."

"The earls must be arrested then," Leicester said.

"Easier said than done, my lord." Walsingham shook his black head. "They are holed up in their castles and will not easily be winkled out. I have private information that they are arming in preparation for a winter campaign. The southern counties are weakened by the recent months of plague and — "

"Give me good news," Elizabeth interrupted. "What steps have you already taken?"

"Set a double guard about Milord Norfolk's estate, and drawn up warrants for the arrests of the earls and of Sir Robert Norton."

"The late Lord Latimer's brother? Is he still alive?"

"Past seventy and eager to ride out in what he sees as a sacred cause."

"The old fool." She shook with indignant laughter. "Well, let him bear his banner, but the earls must be arrested as soon as they poke their noses out of their domain. And my cousin of Norfolk must be lodged in the Tower where he will find it rather more difficult to plot and plan."

"What of the Queen of Scots?" Leicester asked. "If she were not here there would be no focus for rebellion."

"You would have me give her safe conduct into France?"

"I would have you execute her," he said.

"I am bound to agree," Cecil said heavily. "The lady is a danger."

"Mr Walsingham, is there proof in any of the letters she has written to Milord Norfolk that she plots my death?"

"No direct proof," he said reluctantly, "but she promises her 'sweet Norfolk' that she will bestow the Crown Matrimonial on him when she comes into her own."

"Were that sad day ever to dawn," Leicester said vehemently, "she would not leave Your Grace long alive."

"I will not kill one who is both my cousin and an anointed queen," Elizabeth said.

"That does credit to your heart but not your head," Cecil said bluntly. "Even the lady Jane had to die when rebellion on her behalf broke out in your sister's time."

Elizabeth shivered, remembering her young cousin, whose nearness to the throne had forced Queen Mary to order her execution. The act had been deemed necessary, but her sister had paid dearly for it with months of agonized conscience pangs. Yet if Jane had not died Elizabeth herself might have been sacrificed and never come to the throne.

"I will not execute the Queen of Scots," she said obstinately. "Treble her guard at Tutbury, and send word through the kingdom that men must prepare to withstand attack from the north. As to the question of my marriage, let us postpone any negotiations until we have dealt with these malcontents." Rising she held out her hand to Leicester who came at once, his darkness a foil for her pale brightness as they passed from the Council Chamber.

"If you took me as husband I would soon set the north to rights on your behalf," he said.

"And have Mary of Scots discreetly murdered? No, Robin, I wish that it could be so, but your reputation does not stand high in the realm."

"May I remind you that like Mary Stuart I also have never been proved guilty?" he said, withdrawing his hand from her clasp.

"I must consider public opinion nonetheless," she insisted. "It is not only the matter of Amy's death but you are the son of that same Warwick who tried to set my cousin, Jane Grey, on the throne and was justly beheaded for it. And grandson to that lawyer executed by my late father for extortion."

"Several of your own relations have ended headless too," he said dryly.

"The case is different. Go and amuse yourself elsewhere, my lord, and leave me be."

He had trespassed too close to that wall behind which her mother gushed blood from a severed neck. Too wise to protest or frame an apology he bowed and walked back towards the Council Chamber.

Looking after him she bit her lip in vexation. Robin refused to accept the fact that a marriage between them was out of the question. He was the son and grandson of attainted men, widely believed to have ordered the murder of his own wife, unpopular because of his close friendship with her and his own arrogance. Somewhere inside her a voice whispered that she clung to these excuses as a means of avoiding marriage, but she mentally shook her head at the insidious whisper and walked on briskly, turning her thoughts to Norfolk's treachery and the danger from the north.

It was a danger that grew and gathered as the months chilled into winter. She had hoped for harsh weather that would make the roads impassable, but though there were flurries of snow and threat of more to come the roads remained open and the marchers plodded south, with the ageing and gallant figure of old Sir Richard at their head.

"More than ten thousand fools to cry for Mary Stuart and the Pope," Kat Ashley marvelled.

"As if I were a tyrant," Elizabeth said, chafing the palms of her hands together as they warmed themselves at the fire. "Do men never learn?"

It seemed not. Though few joined the rebels as they marched on into Durham yet still they came travelling behind the old man who carried the banner of the five wounds.

At New Year the Duke of Sussex struck, moving his well-trained and disciplined men up to meet the ragged band of Stuart and Norfolk supporters, pitting steel and gun against club and arrow.

"All fled and broken, Your Grace," Sussex said with an air of satisfaction at the next Council Meeting.

There were murmurs of approbation around the table.

"Without many casualties among your own men, I hope?" Elizabeth said.

"Very few, I thank Your Grace." Sussex's broad high-coloured face was beaming.

"The leaders?" She tapped her fingers.

"The earls are fled," he admitted. "Northumberland into Scotland but I have word that the Scots will permit us to extradite him. Westmoreland is gone to Flanders. We have Sir Richard Norton in custody."

"Release him," Elizabeth said shortly. "He's an old fool, no more, with a thirst for martyrdom that I'll not gratify. When Northumberland is returned to our realms have him executed. I will teach those upstart northern earls that I am true queen. Have you prisoners from among the commons?"

"Four thousand held at Durham," he told her.

"Hang every fifth man as a warning to the others and let the rest go back to their houses."

"Your Grace tempers justice with mercy," Walsingham said.

"So would I always," she said briefly. "If that is all — ?"

"Milord Norfolk was chief architect

of this rebellion," Leicester said.

"He is in the Tower and took no active part beyond tacit encouragement," she objected.

"Your Grace, tacit encouragement to treason is itself treason," Walsingham said. "Had he been at large he'd have ridden with the rest."

"He is my cousin." Her mouth had set obstinately.

"Did he have cousinly sentiments towards you when he proposed to the Queen of Scots?" Cecil asked the question slyly, his face impassive.

"I do not fit my actions to the actions of others," she retorted.

"Your Grace, Milord Norfolk has naught but weakness and treachery in his nature," Leicester argued.

"Perhaps I ought to emulate him then? Is that what you advise?"

"I would not presume to advise," he said, taking warning from the arching of her plucked brows.

"I have determined to let my cousin go free as a mark of my clemency," she announced, and held up her hand as a chorus of protest, muted but vociferous, broke out. "The duke has told me in a private letter that he regrets ever having been seduced into believing that he had a duty to wed the Queen of Scots or try to restore the Papacy. He has craved my pardon and swears never to offend again."

"You may live to regret that decision," Leicester warned.

"I think not." Her tone had chilled as it often did when he used any voice of authority to her. "It is at all events my personal decision. Northumberland you may have and welcome, but my cousin will have the opportunity to live loyal to me in future."

"She draws back when the moment comes to slay blood kin," Cecil murmured as she swept out with no inviting hand stretched to Robin.

"I know the duke," Walsingham said tensely. "He is as unstable as water."

"Then we shall keep close watch on him," Walsingham said, looking round for agreement. "It would be sad pity if our merciful queen were to find her clemency turned into a dagger that points again at her own throat."

Their voices, lowered discreetly, yet reached the queen's sharp ears as she slowed her step. They were good men and devoted to her though they seldom agreed among themselves. They were politicians all, regarding the execution of a traitor duke as in the normal if unfortunate sequence of events. Even Robin could not guess at the cold horror that gripped her at the thought of shedding the blood of a close relative.

The thought of Leicester brought a deeper frown to her brow. He spoke to her sometimes in public these days as she permitted him to speak to her in private, as if they were equals in more than their ages. It was a habit into which he had fallen and she was foolish to allow it to continue. Cecil had hinted to her more than once that the suitors who offered for her were anxious lest they arrive to find a quasi-king already in England.

She was alone, a rare treat in a Court where there were always attendants scrambling after her to do her bidding, to pick up the ribbons and spangles that frequently came loose from her garments in her rapid progress from room to room, to wait the chance to beg a favour. Today, however, the damp air had kept the ladies within doors and she had left the Council early without escort. The winter held no terrors for her since the cold invigorated her more than the hot winds of summer. She stepped out briskly into the garden, threading her way through the preached alleys against which bare branches splayed themselves in readiness for spring.

She was not after all alone. Out of the corner of her eye she discerned a tall gentleman who kept pace with her, his cloak wrapped about him.

"Come here, if you please." She raised her voice, beckoning him, and as he leaped across the intervening box hedge her memory supplied a name. "It is Hatton, is it not? Christopher Hatton?"

"I am overcome that Your Grace remembers me," he said, dropping at once to his knee. It would be difficult to forget such comely features, she thought, studying the handsome face with the crisply curling fair hair and the blue eyes now regarding her with a look in which she easily recognized hero-worship.

"You are newly come to Court, are you not? In whose service?"

"Yours," he answered, so promptly that she was startled into a laugh.

"Of course. As all my subjects are," she nodded, "but in whose immediate service?"

"Master Cecil, Your Grace. I am newly qualified as lawyer and he was kind enough to offer to stand my patron."

"You could not have a better," she approved. "Yes, I recall you clearly now. You were dancing the latest measure the other night, most gracefully too. Is that now a requirement for lawyers?"

"Not officially, Your Grace." He showed excellent teeth in a smile that made his blue eyes dance. "However it seems to me that quick and nimble wits are required both for lawyers and dancers."

"I concur with your opinion." She motioned him to rise, pleased to find that he was slightly taller than she was. It was a pity that he was fair. She had always preferred dark men, but his face was certainly handsome with character in the firm chin under the short blond beard. His garments were well cut and of good cloth but modestly trimmed.

"Then I shall hold to it, Madam," he said, "since I regard you as the wisest woman in the world."

"Do you so?" For an instant she was almost disappointed in his flattery for it savoured of the sort of compliments she received every day, but his expression was open and honest. An honest lawyer would be an interesting novelty, she thought.

"And I do not believe I shall live to own myself mistaken," he said.

"Walk with me, Master Lawyer." She nodded at him pleasantly, laying her hand on his arm. "I shall pose you a problem, a hypothetical one. If a thief tells me that he plans to rob my house and I lock him up and then his friends come and try to rob my house, is he equally guilty?."

"If the contemplated theft is one theft to be carried out by all and is then delayed because of the detention of the first thief then he is still guilty of having plotted the theft but not of actual involvement," he said promptly. "There might be argument for clemency there."

"How if the thief had not confessed but been discovered in the planning?"

"There might still be grounds for clemency if it could be proved that he had been led into the planning of the crime by evil companions. Your Grace is speaking of Milord Norfolk."

Elizabeth nodded.

"Then you have already decided to give him clemency and, being queen, are above any law. Your decision in any particular case automatically becomes law."

"By God, I wish you'd convince my councillors of that!" she exclaimed.

"Surely Master Cecil does not contradict Your Grace's decisions?"

"Not very often. So you think clemency is in order for Milord Norfolk, do you?"

"I think his offence deserving of the highest penalty," he replied, "but I also believe that Your Grace's impulse to show mercy must waken the most loyal gratitude in any heart."

"God grant it be so." She gave him her own most sparkling smile, her fingers tightening on his arm.

"If He does not answer a queen's prayers then the rest of us are in sad case," he said.

"Master Hatton, I like well your

wit." She loosed her grasp briefly to reach up and clap him heartily on the shoulder. "Will you partner me this evening after supper?"

It would do Robin good to have a potential rival looming on the horizon. Not that any other man, however handsome, could edge him from her heart, but it would do no harm to give him a little jolt of insecurity.

"Your Grace, I would be deeply honoured," Hatton said, "but I fear Milord Leicester might take it amiss."

"What has my lord of Leicester to do with my supper partners?" she demanded.

"Rumour has it — " He paused, his fair skin flushing.

"Rumour is a lying jade," she said tersely.

"I place no trust in rumour, but Milord Leicester is said to have a long reach."

"Do you fear he will call you out and fight you as a rival over a couple of dances?" The idea was so enchantingly scandalous that she threw back her head and laughed aloud. "My dear young lawyer — how many are your years? You seem scarcely past boyhood."

"I am thirty-four, Your Grace, and perhaps too old to partner you."

"You look too young. Perhaps I will adopt you. You are wed, of course?"

"But not for love, Your Grace," he said promptly. "Since there was never the least chance of my reaching for a queen I betrothed myself to the law and until now have proved faithful to her."

An unmarried man was good fortune indeed. There would be no jealous wife to keep at bay, no threat of any sudden and suspicious death.

"You may remain faithful to your Lady Law," she said, "for I am a maiden yet and will not hold out any promise that I cannot keep, but for company and friendship — will you be my partner in that too?"

"Most willingly, Your Grace." He bowed low, kissing her hand.

Out of the corner of her eye she glimpsed the furred cloak of Leicester approaching. She kept Christopher Hatton at her side just long enough to ensure that Robin saw him and then tapped him gently on the cheek.

"Until this evening then. I look forward to the dance."

"Who the devil's that popinjay?" Leicester asked, joining her as Hatton went.

"No popinjay, Rob, but a most witty and charming lawyer new come to Court. His name is — "

"Hatton," Leicester interrupted, snapping his fingers. "Dances like a professional. I marked him the other night."

"You will have the opportunity of marking him again tonight then," Elizabeth said sweetly. "He is to partner me in the dancing after supper."

"Oh?" The sudden stillness in his dark face told her that he had snatched the bait. After a moment he said casually, "Well, I'll not grudge him an

61

evening. He will think himself greatly honoured."

"He will be greatly honoured," she corrected, still sweet. "Or do you begin to look upon my favour as something to be taken for granted? It would be a mistake to do so."

"I never could do that, Bess," he said, so humbly that her heart turned over with love for him but she said only,

"Look to it that you do not, my lord."

3

AFTER raging for two years the plague was sufficiently abated to permit Her Grace to enter London again. The occasion would be marked by the opening of a trading mall on Cornhill where merchants could gather in comfort to transact their business instead of huddling in Lombard Street or under the echoing dome of St Paul's.

"They will be pleased to have me in my capital again, I think," Elizabeth said. There was a faint doubt underlining the complacency of her tone. News of the hangings in Yorkshire and Lancashire had filtered south and, while the suppression of the rebellion was greeted with relief, there were those to mutter that common folk who had followed their lords ended up dead while the chief instigator of the whole sorry affair had been restored to liberty.

"Listen to the cheering and hear the answer," Leicester said.

It was a dull roar, beating in waves against the ancient walls of the city. There had been a sudden cold snap at Yuletide which had chased away the last of the plague and frost glittered along the eaves of the houses and rimed the puddles in the ditches.

She was riding in a litter, the better to display her wide skirts of brocaded silver, the tight bodice sewn with diamonds that dipped into a point at waist level whittling her midriff to nothing, the high collar of silver lace that haloed her curled red hair. Silver outlined her eyes and the cold air had brought a rose flush to her delicately powdered cheeks.

Leicester, riding alongside on his favourite bay, frequently leaned to exchange a few words with her. He looked handsome and arrogant though she noticed that, unlike herself, he was beginning to thicken round the waist. A trifle waspishly, since his years matched her own, she said,

"You eat too much, Robin. You ought to take more exercise."

"Has Your Grace developed a taste for half-starved fledglings?" he countered, glancing towards the youth who rode at the other side of the litter.

Elizabeth stifled a chuckle, glancing at him from beneath her lashes. "Surely you are not jealous of Milord Oxford?" she questioned lightly. "The earl is but newly returned from his honeymoon with Ann Cecil."

"Whom he likes about as well as I like my dog and treats rather less kindly," Leicester said sourly. "He couldn't wait to return to Court where he can spend his time running races with Hatton with yourself as the prize."

"Rob, you are absurd," she said in delight. "Hark, now you shall truly hear the pleasure of the citizens."

Her voice was drowned in the roar of welcome from a thousand throats as the procession entered the nearer gate and began the slow ascent to Cornhill where the magnificent edifice donated to the city by Sir Thomas Gresham had just been completed, its shops filled with goods, its walls and windows hung with coloured lanterns that cast rays of rainbow light over the faces of the crowd.

Stepping from the litter to be greeted by Sir Thomas Elizabeth wondered fleetingly how it might be to be a member of that crowd, not part of the glittering procession but looking at it from the outside. Those who craned their necks to see over the staves of the officers of the Watch would glimpse little more than a flash of silver beneath a pale, translucent oval crowned with red gold hair. For some it would be the one time in their lives when they saw the queen. She imagined they would remember it, and turning towards where the mob surged let her arms open in an unmistakeable embrace.

Then she was entering the covered mall with its paved floors, its dozens of stalls and tiny shops, its rows of bowing, beaming merchants.

"It is magnificent, Sir Thomas." Her face glowed as she addressed him. "You have rendered a great service to the City of London. The increase of trade is one matter very near to my heart. Did you know that my maternal great grandfather was once Lord Mayor of London?"

That had been flung as a gibe upon Anne Boleyn, to remind her of her low birth. Her daughter secure in the knowledge that her lineage on the paternal side was of almost impeccable royal descent prided herself on her merchant forbears.

"I've heard it said that Your Grace could increase the exports twice over if the trade of the country were in your capable hands," Sir Thomas said.

"You heard true," she said, pleased. "It is my firm conviction that if a country spends money on food and grain and woollen cloth it will in the end serve better than gold flung away on arms. Unfortunately some of my advisers are more warlike than myself."

"God grant us many more years of peace," Sir Thomas said.

He had expected his monarch to take a cursory look at the building, pause perhaps to accept a bouquet from the small daughter of one of the stallholders. Elizabeth, however, insisted on walking at a snail's pace round the entire complex of stone and wood and glass. She often paused to speak to the shopkeepers who clustered at their doors, or called upon one of her entourage to carry some trifle that had been pressed upon her. When she finally emerged into the open again she was holding the small girl who had shyly presented the bouquet by the hand, and laughed with her attendants as the waiting crowd cheered again, one wag yelling above the other voices,

"Give us an heir, bonny Queen Bess!"

"That would be gift indeed," Sir Thomas said.

"A generous sentiment." There was a softness in her glance as she recalled that this fine donation had been made in memory of his own dead son. "However, first I must get me a husband. I fear that when I do the entire country will be jealous."

"With good cause, for it is likely that Your Grace will take a foreign bridegroom and be absent for part of the year," he said.

"Lord forbid that I should run around in foreign lands to keep my husband in view! We are to sup at your house, are we not?"

"Modestly, I fear." Helping her into the litter under the bright lanterns he found himself hoping that all would go smoothly. His cook had made extensive and secret enquiry into the dishes Her Grace best liked, and a bedchamber had been repanelled and hung with silk lest she choose to spend the night there.

Her Grace was, fortunately, in excellent mood. Sir Thomas was complimented upon his elegant mansion in Bishopsgate, upon the fine supper laid before his guests on his Venetian crystal, on the good citizenship he had so amply demonstrated with his donation.

"Which I shall name the Royal Exchange," Elizabeth informed him as the pleasantly convivial supper drew to a close. "I shall have letters patent drawn up to register the name. From this time forward the merchants of London shall act under royal patronage."

"We have a wise monarch," Cecil said, applauding gently.

"You have a monarch who is not afraid to reward excellence." She smiled across the table at her chief minister, thinking that of them all he had always been most loyal, even to doing what lay in his small power to help when he had been a mere clerk and she a friendless princess. "I intend to create you a peer, Cecil. Will you accept a lordship?"

"With humility and gratitude, Your Grace." His quiet face had flushed with pleasure.

"What title will you take?" She looked a question.

"Whatever it pleases Your Grace to bestow," he replied promptly.

"Be Lord of Burleigh then." The speed of her own response proved that she had already made her decision. "I will confirm you in the lands and pension thereof."

"Your Grace, good things come in threes," the Earl of Oxford said boldly. The heavy-lidded sea-coloured eyes turned lazily in his direction. An amusing puppy, she thought, and bored with his plain, clever young wife. But of late he had begun to ask too often for small favours that were tending to grow larger.

"You are right," she said aloud, "and so I bestow a third gift. Christopher

Hatton, you shall have a knighthood and be the captain of my guard. There, now I have given my three gifts."

Oxford's vapid, good-looking countenance had fallen. In a moment he would say something peevish and disrespectful.

"I thank you on behalf of my protégé since he seems to have lost the use of his tongue." The newly created Lord Burleigh spoke smoothly, forestalling any remark contemplated by his discomfited son-in-law.

"I am spellbound," Hatton said simply.

"The captain of my guard bewitched? Lord forbid," Elizabeth said merrily. "Sir Thomas, this has been a happy occasion and I am loth to leave but — "

"If Your Grace has a mind to stay," Sir Thomas said eagerly, "a chamber is prepared."

"Unhappily I must continue on to Westminster." Her sigh was genuine since of all her palaces she found

Westminster the most draughty and uncomfortable. "Keep that chamber against the day when I shall have leisure to sleep in it."

"It will be kept ready for use at a moment's notice," he promised recklessly. Elizabeth gave him her hand and entered the litter, wincing suddenly as a stab of pain shot through the calf of her leg. She had scraped it against the corner of her chair some days before and forgotten it almost, the graze having been slight.

"You are generous with your honours tonight," Leicester observed, riding close at her side.

"You do not grudge Cecil a lordship?"

"He and I are generally at outs," he grimaced, "but he serves you well. But why make Hatton the captain of your guard. He's a fool of a lawyer."

"He's a lawyer but no fool," she retorted. "The post will give him some security. He is not wealthy, and it will irritate Oxford. That young man becomes importunate."

"And sometimes you choose to give."

"Not as much as I have ever given to you," she said earnestly, leaning to catch at the trappings of his mount through the side of the swaying litter. "Never to any man, my Rob, I swear it."

"But you could have done," he said, "if you had agreed to marry me."

"Oh, cease grumbling." She gave his leg a sharp buffet and withdrew into the litter, raising her hand now to one side, now to the other, as she glimpsed groups of cheering citizens in the gaps between her attendant riders.

Westminster was as draughty as she remembered and she was too tired to sleep. Crowds had always stimulated her, making her feel young and lively.

"Which I am still," she said aloud, dismissing her tiring women and easing her foot onto a low stool. The ominous shaft of pain came again and she bit down on her lower lip.

"What ails my loveling?"

For all that she was nearly sixty Kat

Ashley had eyes like a hawk where her former charge was concerned.

"A nothing. I grazed my leg the other day."

"Did you tell the physician?" Kat demanded.

"For a mere scratch that a child might get in climbing a wall?"

"Is that what you were doing?"

"I banged into something. Look, it's only a — "

She had pulled up her skirt as she spoke and rolled down her stocking. Queen and lady-in-waiting stared together at the pistule that had formed in the centre of the bruise.

"I'll get the physician," Kat said at last.

"Not now." Elizabeth reached up, holding her fast by her sleeve. "What rumours do you think will start if you go running through the court at midnight looking for my physician?"

"I shall stroll if it pleases you better," Kat said acidly, "but that ulcer needs to be dressed."

"It is a blister, not an ulcer," Elizabeth said.

An ulcer was what her father had developed in middle years when his brawny handsomeness was turning to fat and the pox beginning to make its inroads upon his body and brain. He had deserved the pox with his six wives and his lights of love, but she was virgin still. No man could have infected her.

"A blister," Kat agreed, her glance quick and comprehending. "We'll let Doctor Phipps have a look at it tomorrow. No great hurry now I see it properly."

"I have always been rapid to heal," Elizabeth said. "Why this?"

"All children heal quickly," Kat said. "You are no longer a child, that's all."

"Neither am I an old woman," Elizabeth said.

"Nobody would take you for thirty-eight and that's a fact," Kat agreed.

"You know perfectly well that I'm thirty-seven — oh, you — Ash Cat."

Elizabeth's face broke into laughter and she flung a cushion in her companion's direction.

She was in the summer of her life and the pistule on her leg was only a blister. The age-old spectre that stalked through her nightmares retreated. King Harry lowered his stinking hulk of body back into its unregretted grave.

"The graze was not properly washed at the time it occurred, Your Grace," Doctor Phipps said in his severe manner the following day. "There is some dirt got into the wound. I shall foment it and order you to rest your leg upon a stool for a week. It will heal swiftly."

"You are certain?" She lowered her voice, her eyes on his bent head as he dealt with lotion and bandage.

"Permit me to recognize a simple blister when I see one," he said, offended.

"It is not ulcerated?" She hesitated over the word.

"A blister caused by dirt getting into the wound though the hurt itself was very slight. I have noticed that frequently happens if the skin is broken and is not washed at once. An ulcer, Your Grace, is caused by that which arises from evil humours in the blood. This is not such."

"So, this gives me a reason to idle by the fire." Her voice was gay again and her face was rosy. Nightmares were only nightmares and seldom turned to reality.

There was unfortunately no way of hiding her indisposition since, despite the physician's reassurances, the blister obstinately refused to heal, but remained angry and swollen.

"If I cannot hide it then I will advertise it," she said ruefully. "If I am honest about this hurt then at least there will be no exaggerated whispers."

But the forced inactivity fretted her energetic spirit. She, who adored dancing and walking and riding, was compelled to sit quietly while the others danced. Her condition had its advantages however. She could take note which of those who swore eternal devotion actually spent the long spring evenings at her side, amusing her with conversation, and who still danced with other people.

Oxford was one of those who danced, unwilling to relinquish his pleasures in order to sit at her side. Hatton did not dance, but companioned her evening after evening, insisting that he too had an aching limb and was glad of the rest.

"He truly loves you," Kat said. "There is never any whisper of any other woman."

"Meaning?" Elizabeth looked at her sharply.

"That Milord Leicester has a light of love."

"Douglas Sheffield, Lord Howard's girl," Elizabeth said indifferently. "She is twenty years old and married to an old man. Rob merely seeks to give her some amusement."

"You are grown very tolerant," Kat said dryly.

"I anticipated that Robin would enjoy other women from time to time," Elizabeth said. "I will not grant him all that he craves and he is no monk. His passing amours cannot touch what we have. He and I know that."

"Oh, if only you would accept him as husband," Kat said wistfully. "He has loved you for so long."

"I will not marry a subject," Elizabeth said obstinately. "Especially will I not marry a subject suspected of having his wife murdered."

"That was years ago," Kat protested. "Nobody except yourself even considers it now. Why, if you took Milord Leicester there is nobody in the land who would speak against it."

"Cecil mistrusts him still."

"Let Milord Burleigh keep to his politicking and leave your private life alone," Kat said.

"Ash Cat, you are the complete romantic," Elizabeth said, laughing. "Don't you understand that a queen cannot have a truly private existence, since all that she does affects the realm? Oh, if it were my choice entirely I would wed Robin tomorrow, but the truth is that for the safety of the realm I must make a foreign alliance."

"With Anjou?"

"With Anjou," Elizabeth said. "The new alliance between France and Spain is a threat to our own security. We must make it a triple alliance and Anjou is the key." She broke off, seeing Walsingham's tall, stooping figure hove into view.

"I will go and chivvy the maids," Kat said, rising somewhat hastily for she disliked the minister.

"Come and sit down," Elizabeth said hospitably as he bowed. She was mischievously aware that though he was happily married Walsingham had an inclination towards his own sex, which made his fulminations against Anjou's habits ironically amusing.

"Your Grace's limb amends?" He seated himself on a stool, awkwardly stretching out his long legs.

"It is very much better since it was poulticed," she assured him. "From the look on your face my recovery doesn't seem to please you?"

"I am delighted, Your Grace," he answered gloomily, "but I wish the improvement had occurred sooner."

"Why so do I," she assured him, smiling. "It is a great grief to be laid up with a — but you are not here merely to enquire after my health. What bodes?"

"A letter from Anjou," he said.

"Ah, my laggard suitor at last rouses himself to write to me. What's ill about that?"

"The letter is not to Your Grace," he said. "The duke wrote to his mother, Catherine."

"So this is a copy. I will not ask who made it. Your ways are your own ways and keep me most minutely informed. What says the duke to his lady mother?"

"That nobody asked his opinion before these marriage negotiations began, and that he will not be married without his consent to — to an old creature with a sore leg."

For a moment Elizabeth's face was still. Then it flamed scarlet. "'An old creature with a sore leg'," she quoted. "Those were his words?"

"His exact words, Your Grace." And Francis Walsingham would repeat the exact words, hitting out at the sex he despised even though he served her loyally.

"I am not yet forty and I have a blister on my leg which is healing," she said, the scarlet blanching to white. "How dare he slander me thus?"

"It was a private missive, not intended for other eyes," he told her. "I felt that you ought to be told of it that you might be made aware of his true sentiments concerning this union."

"You were correct. I'd not wish to marry a man who holds me secretly is such contempt."

"But an alliance with France would

be most valuable," he said.

"I will write to Queen Catherine," she said slowly. "I will regret that Anjou is so ill informed that he imagines me to be old and crippled, and I will assure Catherine that I do not hold her at fault for her son's ignorance. Draft me such a letter to sign, Walsingham."

"You carry the argument into the opposite camp, placing them in the wrong, and also showing yourself to be wise and calm, not swiftly to temper," he approved.

"Am I not?" She gave an angry little laugh. "I am so furious that I could spit, my friend, but of what use is spitting when Anjou sits out of range? Go and see to it, or have you more pleasant tidings for me?"

"Only that the Pope has ratified the excommunication of yourself."

"So I am flung out of a Church to which I never wanted to belong." She shrugged, but her face had darkened.

"The wording of the Bull is such that any of your Catholic subjects might feel justified in rebelling against you in favour of the Queen of Scots."

"They will not," she answered. "Even my Catholic subjects don't want the Inquisition in this land. Their personal loyalty to me is beyond question."

"What of the north, where the Papists are most numerous?"

"The peasants there were hanged for joining a rebellion against their lawfully anointed queen, not for their religious views. They will not rise again."

"I hope Your Grace's confidence is justified," Walsingham murmured.

"I know my people," she said. "They will remain loyal save for a few malcontents who would be malcontent whoever sat upon the throne. Go and write to Queen Catherine."

"Your Grace." Rising and bowing he backed away.

"An old creature with a sore leg," she repeated aloud. The sentence stung and enraged her. Well, Catherine de Medici would be placed in the embarrassing position of having to apologize for her son's opinions of the queen who condescended to consider marriage with him.

Meanwhile she must make every effort to appear in public, beautiful, gracious and above all healthy. She pulled up the hem of her skirt and examined her leg anxiously. The putrid matter had been drained from it and the surrounding skin looked less angry. When she walked it gave her only an occasional twinge. From now on she would resume regular exercise.

There was an outburst of applause when, after supper that evening, she rose, holding out her hand to Leicester and saying, "This evening, Robin, I am well enough to dance again."

"I have missed you as a partner these past weeks," he said under cover of the clapping.

"Not sufficiently to sit with me for long periods." She pouted slightly.

"Good Lord, Bess." He grinned at her unrepentantly. "Since when was I content to sit like one of your lapdog admirers? Were we married I swear I'd never stray from you, but we are not, and even you, whom I love more than my life, cannot command all my time."

"Some of that time you spent with Douglas Sheffield," she could not resist saying as they began the slow measure.

"Howard's daughter? She is bored and lonely and the old fellow her father married her to is on his last legs. I took pity on her now and then."

"While you were taking pity on Douglas Sheffield," Elizabeth said sweetly, "I was bestowing Ely Palace on Hatton."

"What!" He almost missed a step, correcting himself instantly but frowning at her. "The bishop's palace? he will not readily yield it."

"He did not." A faint smile curved her mouth. "He grumbled mightily that the palace went hand in hand with his bishopric and that he held it in trust for his successor. I wrote that as I had appointed him so I could unfrock him, unless he packed his bags and found a more modest dwelling."

"So Hatton will have a palace now." Leicester's frown had deepened. "You pile too many favours upon him."

"I pile my favours on whom I please," she answered sharply. "If you had sat with me hour and hour together to cheer me while my leg was sore why, you might have had a palace too. Oh, don't look so sulky, my sweet Robin. Just as it means nothing to you when you flirt with silly girls, so it means nothing to me to bestow a small palace here and there on a man who does love me."

"But you have no feeling for him? You haven't, have you?"

"I find him both honest and charming," she said, suppressing a small cry of pain as she put too much weight on her leg in the turn at the end of the long chamber.

"And I am not?"

"You are the man I love," she said softly. "Never doubt that, Robin,

Hatton and Oxford amuse me and the former will do me good service, I feel certain of it. But you and I cannot be separated. Don't you know that?"

"And you will not consent to our being joined either." The measure was ending and he escorted her to her place. "You will make a match with that fool, Anjou, who is incapable of loving any woman as she ought to be loved, let alone a woman like you."

"Oh, Anjou is not so happy about the marriage either." She leaned to whisper what Francis Walsingham had read and was delighted to see a vein swell in Leicester's brow.

"That French catling should be horsewhipped," he growled.

"Oh, his lady mother will send apology for her son's bad opinion of me," Elizabeth assured him. "Have no fear that I will forget the insult. But personal considerations cannot be allowed to interfere with state policies.

A marriage with France will give us some security against those who would put Mary Stuart on my throne and bring back Papacy."

"The most of your Catholic subjects are loyal, I'd swear," he said.

"So would I, Robin. So would I." She pressed his hand smilingly, her eyes on his handsome face. Yet she was conscious of the gaze of Oxford who glowered in his seat and of Hatton hopefully waiting to be noticed again.

"Will you dance again tonight?" Leicester was enquiring.

"I will not try my strength over much," she decided prudently. "You have my leave to go and flirt with Douglas Sheffield who is staring at you as if she would like to eat you up."

"If you are sure?" He kissed her hand and her cheek, and rose from his knee. She tried not to notice that there was eagerness in his dark eyes.

A month later she sat in Council, her long fingers tapping irritably as

Walsingham made his report.

"The Queen Mother of France has expressed deep regret at the unfortunate comments made by her disobedient son, the Duke of Anjou," he informed the company in his dry, level tones. "She has promised to speak to him most severely about the lack of respect he displays though she points out that the remarks were penned in a private letter not intended for any eyes but her own. She is also delighted to learn that rumour lied and that Her Grace is both healthy and in her usual looks."

"Bitch," Elizabeth said without heat. "Anything more?"

"She wonders if Your Grace might consider her youngest son, Alencon, as a possible husband, if she finds it impossible to bring Anjou to a sense of his duty," Walsingham said.

"Alencon is all of sixteen," Sussex said. "Your Grace would as well adopt as marry him."

"She offers me insult after insult.

Does she think herself so high above retaliation?"

"What kind of action were you considering?" the newly created Lord Burleigh asked.

"There is nothing I can do, as you well know, Cecil." She drummed faster on the table top. "I cannot declare war — don't want to declare war. God knows that is the last path I wish to take. Yet the rumours she lets loose into Europe are damaging."

"Your Grace ought to rise above them," Burleigh said.

"You rise above them!" she retorted. "You are not being described as an old creature with a sore leg."

"They would not trouble to say such things of me since they are too near the truth in my case," he said. There were chuckles about the table. He continued, his tone equable. "Your Grace can take comfort in the fact that these slanders are without foundation. The Duke of Anjou is a foolish boy but you can reserve his spanking until he comes to be your husband."

"From what I hear of Anjou he would enjoy the spanking more than the marriage," Elizabeth said, and saw even Walsingham's dour countenance lift into a grin.

4

NOT even the Duke of Anjou could have denied that the queen was in high good looks and health as she sat, her golden skirts spreading about her, to receive the Scottish delegation. Her skin glowed palely under red hair and her eyes, shadowed artfully with gold, glinted green as she watched the Earl of Morton approach. Mary Stuart's illegitimate half-brother was a handsome man, black-bearded and tall, his voice deep and musical. Of all the Scots lords she had seen she reckoned him the most charming and the most treacherous. Only a man of consummate treachery could have masterminded the downfall of his sister queen and so hidden his part in it that the same queen had exclaimed that he would never have suffered her to be brought to such a pass.

"Greeting, a thousand such on the occasion of Your Grace's birthday," was his opening remark.

"Our thanks to you for that greeting." She inclined her head graciously, noting the tiny smile at the corners of his mouth. He thought her disarmed, a female as foolish as his sister.

"Our mission is one of help," he was continuing.

"Oh?" She arched a questioning eyebrow.

"To relieve Your Grace of the charge of Mary Stuart," he said.

"You refer to the Queen of Scots?"

"The abdicated Queen of Scots."

"Deposed," she corrected softly. "Mary did not give up her crown of her own free will."

"She was not deemed fit to rule," he said, the smile souring.

"Not deemed fit by whom?" Elizabeth asked. "By certain rebel lords among whom I include yourself who took it into their own hands to remove a sacred and crowned monarch from her place."

"A female monarch," Morton said. "Master Calvin has proved that women ought not to rule."

"I am not unacquainted with the ideas of John Calvin. In England we regard him as a fanatic with a great hatred of the female sex."

"In Scotland he is regarded as a great prophet. Master Knox — "

"Is another fanatic," she interrupted. "We pay no account to his views either. What is it you would have of us?"

"The person of my sister," he said, suddenly blunt.

"Your royal sister," she amended, laying faint stress on the second word. "You were born bastard, were you not?"

"I count my lineage as royal as hers."

"The law counts differently," she said. "She is queen and you are — "

"I do not seek to overturn the law," he broke in. "I do not seek the crown for myself."

"I am sure we are all vastly relieved to hear it," she drawled.

"My nephew, King James the Sixth of Scotland is true heir, being the only male issue of Queen Mary and the late King Henry — "

"He means Darnley," Elizabeth said to nobody in particular. "I had forgotten that she gave him the Crown Matrimonial."

"And then had him killed," Morton declared.

"As to that charge we will enquire into it when we have leisure," Elizabeth said.

"In Scotland she will receive a fair trial."

"A queen to be tried like a common criminal by rebel lords and one of them a bastard? You think I could countenance such a proceeding?"

"We do not rebel against the lawful heir of Queen Mary," he argued.

"Ah, yes, little Jamie. He is playing with his wooden soldiers for part of each day, I suppose, or do you keep his nose buried in the words of Calvin and Knox?"

"He is a child of remarkable proclivities, and will be a fine king one day. Meanwhile his Council must rule in his stead, protecting his interests."

"And who is to protect the interests of my cousin, Mary Stuart?" she cried, colour flaring along her cheek bones. "She is a queen and a woman like myself. Am I to hand her over to her murderers without protest?"

"Then bring her to trial yourself," he snapped, his suave manners vanishing. "There are proofs enough of her complicity in her late husband's murder."

"We shall hold an enquiry when the time is ripe," Elizabeth said. "For the moment we have more pressing matters to attend."

"She is a focus of rebellion in your own kingdom, Madam," he argued. "As your heiress — "

"A place in the succession from which my own father removed her."

"King Harry also removed yourself from that same succession," Morton said angrily. "I have not observed Your

Grace hastening to comply with his wishes."

"My father had a habit of altering the succession according to his mood at the time," Elizabeth said, "but on his death bed he restored both my elder sister and myself to the line of heirs. He did not so restore the descendants of his sister, Margaret Tudor, I do, however, agree with you that we cannot regard the actions of my late lamented father as sacrosanct. If I gave Mary to you then I but transfer the focus of disaffection to Scotland, where my writ does not run."

"It is not meet that a female should rule," he said loudly.

The queen's hand banged sharply on the carved arm of her throne. In her pale face her eyes were blazing. "Do you seek to bully me in my own realm as you bullied the Queen of Scots?" she cried. "I am of different mettle, my good lord. Whether she be innocent or guilty is not for a bastard rebel to judge. When time allows we

99

ourselves shall make legal enquiry into the circumstances of Darnley's death, but until then she will remain as a protected guest in my land, for I'll never agree to hand her over to the tender mercies of ravening wolves. And so you may tell the rest of your pack. You are dismissed!"

He had regained his dignity, bowing with exaggerated courtesy, his attendants closing in around him as he withdrew.

"God protect any woman from such a brother," Elizabeth muttered, staring after him.

At her elbow Burleigh said very low, "It might not be wise to alienate the Scottish lords completely."

"So send after him to his lodgings with a handsome present," she said, equally low. "Tell him that the current negotiations with France would preclude my handing over Mary Stuart anyway, though the Lord is witness that I'd not want to yield her into their tender mercies."

"Amen," said Burleigh, though he

immediately added, "Were her existence not such a threat to the security of your realm I would entirely agree."

It was the canker in her side. The Pope had publicly stated that Elizabeth was a bastard, fruit of an illegal and incestuous partnership. She believed that under her mild rule the English Catholics would remain loyal, but there were no guarantees. Not until she was safely wed with a child in her arms would she count herself as safe, and if she wed then she must vanquish once and for all the terrors that beset her at the thought of giving herself completely to any man.

The rich colours of autumn were paling into winter, the leaves crackling underfoot, their sap drained. Now and then a flurry of snow brought hints of a harsh winter ahead.

"The cold weather enlivens me," Elizabeth told La Motte as they paced together in the gardens of Hampton Court. "I like nothing better than a brisk walk on a winter morning."

"Your guest suffers from the cold," the ambassador said.

"I will have extra fires lit in your apartments," she began.

"I speak not of myself but of the Queen of Scots," he said. "She has written to my master to complain of the conditions in which she is held. Tutbury Castle is in an exposed and bitter situation and as she is so seldom permitted to ride out her health is impaired."

"She has courage," Elizabeth said sarcastically, "to complain of her treatment at my hands when she would leap into my place without a second thought should opportunity afford."

"King Charles feels great concern on her behalf and charges me to bring the matter to your attention."

"Very well, you have brought it to my attention," Elizabeth said crossly, walking a little faster. "Let us turn to other matters. The Duke of Anjou is now willing to continue with the marriage negotiations?"

"Queen Catherine brought him to a more amenable frame of mind," La Motte said. "He now says that he was misled by common report into his former opinion of Your Grace, and is prepared to accept that you are both young and comely, which is no less than the truth."

"To speak plainly," Elizabeth said. "I myself am now wavering. That surprises you?"

"Not in the least," La Motte said dryly.

"I know that the marriage of any monarch must be an affair of state." She decided to ignore the dryness. "However I am a woman, Mr Ambassador, and there is in my heart all the longing for affection that a normal woman feels. I would like to see Anjou before I definitely accept him."

"He is genuinely handsome. I myself can assure Your Grace."

"What a man sees as handsome in

his own sex may not be perceived in the same way by a women," she objected.

"I can obtain portraits, Your Grace."

"I have already seen portraits of him," Elizabeth said impatiently. "A portrait may lie. My father chose his fourth wife, Anna of Cleves, on the basis of one of Master Holbein's miniatures," she reminded him. It was not perhaps the best example to take and she seemed to realize it, adding hastily, "Not that I would so insult the duke as to publicly repudiate him were he not to please me. What I had in mind was a private visit, incognito. I myself would be ready to go secretly to some port there to greet my suitor. He also would have the opportunity of seeing me."

"Such a visit could not possibly go unremarked," La Motte said, hiding dismay.

"A young man would look upon it as a splendid adventure, surely?"

"Not the Duke of Anjou," La Motte said.

"Well, sound him upon the matter," she insisted. "To tell you the truth, though my own mind has never inclined much towards matrimony and any union contemplated is for the good of my realm, I hope to inspire affection in my bridegroom and be loved by him in return. You know another gentleman has now offered for my hand?"

"No, Madam, I did not," La Motte stood stock still in consternation.

"My erstwhile suitor, the Archduke Maximillian, who could not wait out five years widowhood but must needs wed while I was still trying to make up my mind, has a son by his first wife."

"Duke Rodolph," the ambassador nodded.

"He has written most charmingly, suggesting the alliance."

"Your Grace cannot be serious," he said, smiling uneasily. "Duke Rodolph is younger than the Duke of Anjou whose youth has caused you so much heart searching."

"I am beginning to think we make altogether too much pother about length of years," she said. "After all most people are agreed that I look youthful — "

"Astonishingly so," he slid in.

"And Anjou is amazingly mature for his age. The ten years between us is accordingly of small account."

They were both perfectly well aware that the gap was nearer twenty, but he let it pass, saying only, "I would be sorry if Your Grace were to join with Austria after all our efforts to persuade you to look with favour in the direction of France."

"Well, we shall see. I have spent a lot of time studying the portraits that I have seen, trying to imagine their subject in motion."

"I will have other portraits sent for Your Grace's perusal," he promised. "May I in return assure my master that the Queen of Scots will be given leave to exercise regularly now that the colder weather is coming, and that the rooms at Tutbury are properly warmed."

"It is a great pity," she commented acidly, "that my affairs are not so often in the mind of your master as Mary Stuart's seem to be. I will treat my guests with more courtesy than would be afforded to me were I in the same position."

"And he must be content with that," she told her Council later in the month. "Mary Stuart is the thorn in my side as you all know, the thorn in all our sides. Any other more ruthless monarch would have had her tried and executed years ago — many of you have urged me to it. But I am mindful of the awe and respect due to a crowned monarch and the affection I owe to a near relative — where is Milord Leicester?"

"He went to Lord Sheffield's funeral," Hatton said.

"I trust the said lord is deceased?"

"Two days ago, Your Grace."

"And I was not told? Why not? Must the older members of my Court drop dead in their tracks one by one without my being informed?"

"Your Grace declared that you liked not to talk of death," Burleigh said.

"Informing me of a death is somewhat different from making it a subject of conversation. Why did Leicester have to go galloping off there?"

"He went as Your Grace's representative," Burleigh told her.

"Did he indeed?" She bit her lip, thinking suddenly of the adoring blue eyes and fair curls of the just widowed Douglas Sheffield.

"Something else troubles Your Grace?" Oxford said.

"There have been most disloyal words spoken in Parliament," she said.

"Surely not, Your Grace." Burleigh looked shocked. "As I recall the members agreed to vote for the subsidies you need."

"Which is why I called a parliament in the first place. It was not part of their duty to dare to criticize my intended marriage."

"I heard no criticism," Sussex said, puzzled.

"They tabled a motion begging me to think twice before I took a bridegroom so many years younger than myself." Her voice shook with outrage. "For years they have urged me to wed when my inclination was against it and now, when I declare myself willing to marry for the sake of the realm, they find fault with my choice as if they had any right to comment upon it."

"Unfortunately they do have that right," Burleigh said, "provided they remain within the limits of the law. The motion was couched in most affectionate and respectful terms."

"I will remove them from the House of Commons until they learn better manners," she fumed.

"Your Grace, you really cannot interfere with the traditional prerogatives of Parliament," Burleigh insisted.

"My father managed well enough without calling a parliament for years," she said. "I would like to have seen his face if any member dared to speak out against any marriage he chose to make."

"Your Grace is then determined upon marriage with Anjou?"

"What is this 'determined'?" she asked. "You speak as if I were some unruly maiden who defies her parents in order to wed. You have been urging me to take a husband for the past ten years. I am fixed upon Anjou, who is young enough to be moulded into a more perfect prince but not so young that he cannot grow into love liking with me. It will be Anjou."

There was a silence for a moment and in that silence she felt all the doubts. At thirty-eight she was still capable of bearing children, but neither so many or so easily as a younger woman, and the suitor she had chosen was not only many years younger than herself but liked his own sex more than he liked women. Their concern was for her, she knew, but it was also for themselves since nothing would be quite the same once there was a king on the throne.

"They ask for several concessions," Burleigh said at last. "The Duke is to be permitted to practise his own Catholic faith. Since that is technically against the law we cannot agree. What he practises in private is his own affair but he must be seen to accompany you to the Anglican services."

There were murmurs of agreement all about the table. Nobody wanted another Philip of Spain who had come with his priests and his intolerance to coax the queen into persecution until Merciful Mary Tudor had become Bloody Mary without ever quite realizing how she had lost the love of her people.

"He wants an allowance of ten thousand pounds a year," Burleigh continued.

"Will Parliament vote so much to him," Sussex asked.

"With little dissent," Burleigh assured them.

"The commons will be relieved to have the threat of France's support of Mary Stuart lifted by this marriage," Heneage commented.

"Anjou demands also the title of king," Burleigh said. "There is no reason for denying him."

"It seems then there is no impediment?" It was Elizabeth who spoke, her eyes slowly scanning the faces about the table. They were so well known to her that she sometimes felt as if they were family — Burleigh's lean and thoughtful countenance, the melancholy twist to Walsingham's mouth, the broad Saxon features of Sussex and Arundel, the clipped reddish beard of Heneage, Hatton with his handsome face turned in her direction as a flower turns to the sun. Leicester ought to have been here. On the day her betrothal was being arranged he had no right to go riding off to a funeral so that he could be on the spot to comfort the pretty young widow. Robin would have found some impediment to delay the marriage. She reminded herself sharply that she was eager to wed. The whole country was eager for her to wed. She must always do her duty by the realm. That was important.

"I see no impediment," Burleigh said.

It was a season for weddings. Three of her younger maidservants had recently taken husbands, and she had danced at their receptions, delighted that the blister on her leg had healed and the sharp pain that had sometimes troubled her had gone.

"Yule will be merry this year," she informed Leicester. "It will be the last time I celebrate it as a maiden lady."

"Am I expected to rejoice that another man is going to enjoy you?" he asked wryly.

"Oh, you can console yourself with little Douglas Sheffield," she teased.

"She begins to bore me," he said. "She thinks everything that issues from

113

my lips is Holy Writ, nodding her head solemnly to the most stupid manner imaginable. She's a tedious young woman."

"I knew I was right not to be jealous," she said, delighted. "Oh, Robin, I tell you truly that if it were my decision alone then I would marry you and leave Anjou in France with his mother, but this French alliance is necessary. There is too much amity between France and Spain."

"Then I must continue to flirt with Douglas?"

"Not on my account." She took his hand, smiling up at him. "Never think that my wedding Anjou or any other man can lessen what we have been and are to each other."

"I know it," he said and would have kissed her, but she broke from his embrace to greet Walsingham who had entered the long gallery where she and Leicester were walking, the rain making outdoor exercise unpleasant.

"Such a day to come to Court, Sir

Francis," she chided. "You had done more wisely to stay at home."

"Unfortunately it was needful for me to come at once," he said in his gloomy fashion.

"You have ill news?" For an instant the possibility that Anjou had dropped dead glowed in her imagination.

"News of treason, Your Grace, in the place where treason was uprooted before."

"Speak plain," she commanded.

"Milord of Norfolk has resumed his correspondence with the Queen of Scots," Walsingham said.

"He would not dare!"

"He has dared, Your Grace. I have the proofs."

"What proofs? What was in this correspondence?"

"Milord Duke used the services of one Ridolfi, a Florentine banker with whom he has had some business dealings in the past. Ridolfi has acted as courier between the duke, the Queen of Scots and the Duke of Alva."

"So Spain is implicated?" She had moved to a seat by one of the long windows and gestured to both of them to be seated. "Go on."

"Alva undertook to land ten thousand men in Scotland who would march across the border, allied with those Scottish lords still loyal to her cause, and pluck her from Tutbury. Then Milord Norfolk would marry her and raise up all English Catholics to place her upon the throne."

"How was this discovered?" Leicester demanded.

"Norfolk sent two thousand pounds to the Scottish lords of Mary Stuart's party by the hand of a courier named Brown — an innocent dupe for he was told it was silver for the duke's private payments. He judged the weight too heavy and broke the seal. When he discovered gold and letters in cipher he had the wit to bring the lot to me. It was a pretty plot and might have gone some way towards success had Brown not acted on his own initiative."

He had recited the events with no more feeling than he would have displayed when reading out a financial report. Leicester had told her once that Walsingham had ice water in his veins. Listening to him Elizabeth had a sudden disquieting picture of his reciting a different set of facts in the same toneless manner to Mary Stuart after some future plot had gone undiscovered.

"What steps have you taken?" She forced herself to speak as calmly as he.

"I have arrested Barker and Banister, two of the duke's henchmen. They seem to be involved as couriers too, and I have dispatched officers to Tutbury Castle to search for further letters though I'll be surprised if they find any. I hope I have Your Grace's approval?"

"You have acted very promptly," she said.

"From whom were the letters?" Leicester asked.

"From Milord Norfolk to the Duke of Alva, thanking him for his offer of assistance and informing him that the Queen of Scots had approved the plans and sent her good wishes."

"Was there anything from Mary herself?" Elizabeth asked.

"We found none yet, Your Grace."

"And she will swear she knows not the contents of the others," Leicester said, frowning.

"Whether she knows of the contents or not is of no importance," Walsingham said indifferently. "She has never relinquished her claim to be the legitimate monarch of this realm, nor ceased to encourage those who would put her on that throne. She is no innocent Jane Gray, caught in a coil not of her devising. She is a subtle and dangerous woman who will not hesitate to strike hard at the lawful mistress of our kingdom when opportunity offers."

"Is Norfolk taken?" Elizabeth asked, diverting attention, albeit briefly, from the Queen of Scots.

"I am here to ask Your Grace to sign the warrant for his arrest," Walsingham said. "He is premier duke and a peer of the realm and cannot be taken up like a common felon."

"I will sign it, of course." She took the parchment, reading it as carefully as if she had never seen a warrant for arrest before. "You prepared this very swiftly."

"Madam, I had it ready against the time when Milord Duke would break his promise and turn traitor again," he informed her.

"You were so sure?"

"Yes, Your Grace. There are some men whose natures are like water, always finding their own low level."

"I must congratulate you," she said dully. "You knew the duke better than I did myself. I would have taken oath that having been forgiven he would have thanked God and remained loyal."

He was her relative, her thoughts ran on. She had always set great value on her relatives, especially those with Howard blood. She had forgiven the duke once, set him at liberty, let her heart rule her head. That was a dangerous course for a queen to follow. Even her sister, Mary Tudor, who had wanted to be on good terms with all the family had been forced in the end to send little Jane Grey to the block.

"Arrest Milord Norfolk on a charge of high treason," she said aloud in a voice as cold as Walsingham's own. "Have him conveyed immediately to the Tower. Milord Burleigh, you will preside at his trial? It must be a fair one. He shall be given every opportunity to excuse himself."

From Burleigh's silence as he bowed his head she knew that he could not imagine any adequate excuse for treason. She wanted to tell him that she was right. What her cousin had done struck at the heart of her.

"Your Grace, there is the matter of the Queen of Scots," Leicester said.

"Not now." She began to rise but his voice held her in her seat. He was not the teasing lover now but one of her gravest councillors.

"This plot which Sir Francis has uncovered was designed specifically to put that woman upon your throne, and by implication to bring about your death — "

"Is it so stated in the letters?"

"Not in plain words," Walsingham said, "but it is implicit."

"But not proved," she said.

"Had the plot succeeded and Mary Stuart been raised to your throne do you think that she would have been nice about your fate?" Leicester demanded. "She has been an ever present danger to you since she arrived in England. If Norfolk is to be tried then so must she be."

"I cannot put an anointed queen on trial."

"It has happened before," Walsingham said unwisely.

Her own mother had been tried

within the Tower for adultery and incest, found guilty by twenty-six peers of the realm. Her own father had signed the death warrant. She couldn't remember who had first told her about her mother's end. Perhaps she had gleaned it from odds and ends of conversation, from the broken phrases that trailed into silence when a small, sharp eared child hove into view.

"Let the Queen of Scots alone," she said, her voice low and strained. "She is eager to snatch at any straw to regain her liberty. Who is to swear that I would not act thus given her circumstances?"

"Your Grace would never have acted in ways that set you in such circumstances," Burleigh said, looking pained.

It was not true. As a child she had once been banished from Court for a whole year for making some ill-timed, forgotten jest about her mother. At fourteen she had loved Tom Seymour so passionately that she had almost yielded herself entirely to him, and as a princess at her sister's Court she had sent secret encouragement to the poet's son, Wyatt, in his rebellion. Yet there was truth in so far as though she had sailed very near the wind she had always stopped short, something cautious and sly in her nature acting as a brake upon her deep desires. Perhaps that was the difference between herself and Mary Stuart. And perhaps that gave her a duty to protect the younger, frailer vessel.

5

HER gifts at that Yuletide had pleased her very much. Any gift always pleased her since in her childhood she had seldom been given anything. However this season the offerings had a personal touch that charmed her.

"Do look, Kat." She drew her old governess to the long table on which the presents were displayed. "Even my cooks have brought me samples of their art to tempt me. This quince tart was baked especially for me by John Smithson who was too bashful to come himself with the offering but sent it by the hand of the butler. I went at once to the kitchen to thank him."

It was another proof of the common touch that she possessed, like her father who even in the days of his decline, when his cruelties were known throughout Europe, could still charm a crowd by recognizing in it a familiar face from the French campaign. Her humourless young brother and her half-sister, Mary, had lacked that quality. Neither had her mother had it. Anne Boleyn had despised the common stock from which she sprang and the London mobs had stood mute to watch her go to her crowning.

"They love you well," Kat said fondly.

"Not everybody." Elizabeth face darkened as she turned aside. "There is no doubt of my cousin Norfolk's treachery. It is proved and admitted."

"Perhaps he is out of his wits?" Kat said hopefully.

"He sees himself as the knight on the white steed who rescues the imprisoned damsel from those who hold her in durance," Elizabeth said. "But he is not insane. Believe me, but he has been planning everything most carefully for a long time. And I cannot tell how many would have joined him had his schemes gone undiscovered."

"Surely hardly any save a few Catholic fanatics." Kat looked shocked.

"I pray that you are right." Elizabeth had sunk into a thoughtful mood, her eyes inward-looking, the pleasure at her gifts dimmed.

"It is a long time since this land was ruled so wisely or so mercifully," Kat said.

"Aye, that's true. Did you know that we'll have to erect a new scaffold on Tower Hill since the old one is falling to pieces? That could not have happened in my father's time."

"Very true," Kat said fervently, and both women laughed.

"The news from France is not good," Elizabeth said, sobering abruptly. "Anjou insists on the right to practise his faith."

"I didn't know the duke was so religious," Kat said dryly.

"He is not," Elizabeth said. "It is an excuse because he mislikes the marriage. He has argued against it from the beginning of the negotiations. Oh, he has some cause. I am so much older than he, but he likes not ladies anyway and would, I believe, argue reasons against any wife."

"Why don't you accept my lord Leicester?" Kat said coaxingly. "You love each other and have for almost twenty years."

"For longer, since we were children," Elizabeth said. "We are husband and wife in all but the act. Nothing will ever separate Robin and me."

"Then take him," Kat urged. "The Privy Council may not like it but they will agree if only out of their great desire to see you wed with an heir. Take him, loveling."

"I cannot." Elizabeth's mouth had tightened against pain. "He is son of that same Dudley who tried to put the Lady Jane upon the throne and grandson to the lawyer who cheated and robbed the people and both were executed for their crimes, and he is widower of Amy Robsart whose death has never been satisfactorily explained. His background and his history speak against him. More than that he is a subject whom I myself raised up. I will wed a man of royal blood, Kat, whose hand carries a treaty to protect us all against the Pope and the Stuart."

"But if Anjou is unwilling?"

"I have sent word to France that as we cannot outrage public opinion by allowing him to hold his mass then it is wiser if we both agree to disagree and monsieur looks elsewhere for a bride."

"But you won't take Leicester?"

"I wish you would learn to listen the first time that I speak," she said, irritated. "Must I go on repeating myself? I will not take Leicester. I will marry some other prince. I am still a rich prize, you know."

"Of course," Kat said hastily. "There will be many princes rejoicing that you have decided not to take France."

"I'll not embarrass you by asking for their names," Elizabeth said wryly. "The truth is that the years are passing and each year makes it less likely that I will bear children. Of all things I would love a child of my own. Children are important, Kat. They teach us that incorruption is still possible in the world, and honesty and all things clean."

She had always taken pleasure in the company of children, perhaps, the older woman thought, because she had never been allowed to be a child herself.

"Leicester'd give you babes," Kat began, but Elizabeth flung away, crying.

"Enough, no more!" She put her hands over her ears, whirling away. "You'll not plead Robin's case to me. You'll keep silent, Ash Cat."

Others were not so easily silenced. The breaking off of the French negotiations on the grounds of Anjou's religious scruples brought the whole question of the queen's marriage into the forefront of discussions again. Burleigh, limping slightly from the gout that afflicted him as winter ice gave way to spring rain, sighed heavily as he regarded his monarch.

"It is imperative that Your Grace takes a husband," he said. "Once you have borne a child these plots and ploys to set Mary Stuart upon the throne will fade like mist in the morning. You are the most valuable match in Europe, Madam, and you must choose."

"From whom?" She arched her plucked brows at him, her fingers restlessly twisting her rings.

He sighed again, for the truth was that the number of suitors was rapidly diminishing. She had played off one against another, made promises and skipped away from them, and the truth was that princes grew weary of such coyness. Those who had so eagerly sought her as a bride on her accession more than thirteen years before had taken wives or were glancing towards Mary Stuart who was still less than thirty and reputed to be more amenable.

"It mislikes me to plead his cause," he said at last, "but there is no strong reason why Your Grace should not take the Earl of Leicester. The old scandal of his wife's death is laid to rest in the minds of the people and though I mistrust him and his line he has given many proofs of his loyalty."

"So have you," she teased. "So have all my Council. Must I wed you all?"

"Our wives might grumble," he said, chuckling, "but Leicester has no wife."

"Neither has Christopher Hatton," she pointed out.

"Your Grace might do worse," Burleigh considered. "He is of lower degree than Leicester, but he certainly loves you sincerely and has a good head on his shoulders."

"He is the most graceful dancer at Court," she said dreamily.

"Then is it to be Hatton?"

"Of course not." Rising, motioning him to stay in his seat, she looked down at him, her face scornfully smiling. "I will never marry a subject, Cecil. You may inform the Council so. You may have it announced in Parliament or cried through the streets. No union can hope to succeed where the wife outranks her husband by so great a degree. I will marry a prince or I will not marry."

"There is the younger prince of France," Burleigh said. "I speak of Alencon."

"Who, at nineteen, is exactly half my age," she snapped. "I've heard tell he is also a dwarf and scarred by the smallpox. Why not go out into the fairs and side-shows and choose some freak for the Queen of England to wed?"

He was tactfully silent, knowing that the trial of her cousin and Anjou's reluctance to wed had contributed to her ill humour.

"Send for a portrait of Alencon," she said at last, "and for a truthful description of him. It can do no harm, though even if he is taller and handsomer than reports have it, he is still too young and, like his brother, a Catholic."

"I understand that he would not

insist in having mass offered on his behalf," Burleigh said.

"So you have been considering Alencon already?" Elizabeth stared at him.

"In the event of your not wedding the Earl of Leicester," he said.

"I will not, but I will tell him so myself. He has earned that much for his long loving."

It was not a task she relished. Though she had discussed many possible suitors with him she had always known that he still hoped she would change her mind and bestow upon him the Crown Matrimonial. If she did even those members of her Council who distrusted him as an upstart would accept her decision.

She told him the next day, holding herself very still and composed as she informed him in more polite and formal terms than she generally used to him that after long thought she had decided to issue an announcement that she would never marry a subject.

"You have been telling me for years that you won't marry me," he said. "Why must there be a public announcement about it now? To shame me?"

"To tell the world how greatly I value and love you," she said.

"By not marrying me? Your mind works in a peculiar way."

"If I don't marry you there will always be those to point the finger and say that, in the end, I could not trust you sufficiently to become your wife. I wish to make it absolutely clear that were I free to consult only my heart you would be the man I would choose, but for the sake of my realm I must make a foreign alliance."

He was silent for a long moment, his eyes lowered. She braced herself for an outburst of reproaches, for the accusation that he had stayed single after Amy's death for her sake, but when he did speak his voice was quiet.

"Do you remember how when we were both children of eight we stood together in the gardens of Greenwich and watched the royal barge taking Queen Katheryn to the Tower?"

"The Lightsome Queen." She too spoke quietly, repeating the nickname the common folk had given to King Harry's fifth wife. "She was always laughing and dancing, giving me little gifts, seating me next to her at the high table. Yes, I remember her."

"We both watched her," Leicester said. "She was clad in black, huddled like a trapped thing, and you said to me then, 'I will never marry.' Do you remember that?"

"You cannot hold against me something uttered when I was a child of eight," she said. "Why, of course I shall marry — a prince who will bring us a great alliance and give me heirs. Of course I shall marry, Rob."

"Without loving me less?"

"Oh, Robin!" She shook her head at him, her eyes tender. "I will always love you more than any other man. Must you ask me such a question? I will love you and you will love me. You will not cease from loving me, will you?"

He was silent for so long that an icy finger touched her heart. Then he said sadly,

"No, Bess, I will never cease from loving you."

So now she was free to begin negotiations with Alencon who might prove more amenable than his older brother. The announcement once made could not be withdrawn. She would not now wed the man she loved. Mingled with her sorrow was a curious feeling of relief. It was in that mood that she sent for the death warrant drawn up for Milord Norfolk and put her signature to it firmly. He had been forgiven once but he had betrayed her twice.

That night she dreamed again as she had not dreamed for years, of herself standing at the edge of a platform watching as a tall woman with her black hair piled high knelt down. She knew that the kneeling woman was her mother, but even as she accepted that knowledge the figure changed into the slight frame of her cousin, Jane Grey, blindfolded and hysterical, groping for the block as she cried,

"Help me, please. I cannot find it."

The figure changed again into the shape of Queen Katheryn, wearing the red shoes in which she had danced through more than a year of Elizabeth's childhood. But she had no head, only a stump of neck from which blood spurted, and all those crowding about her on that platform were headless. She put up her hands to her face and felt only the fountain of blood, the jagged flesh where her head had been severed, and woke screaming, sweat matting her hair, her startled ladies rushing in with lamps.

"Send to the Tower." Still trapped in her nightmare she glared round at them. "I am revoking the Duke of Norfolk's execution. Send to the Tower."

No treason deserved that last walk up to that platform of bloodstained straw to join all the spectres of her childhood.

"My cousin of Norfolk will remain in the Tower," she informed her Council the next day. "He will be given ample leisure in which to repent of his foolish passion for the Queen of Scots. Milord Burleigh, have you opened the negotiations with France yet?"

"I have drafted the announcement declaring your intention to lay aside your own desires and match with a foreign prince for the sake of the realm and I have written to Queen Catherine requesting a portrait of her youngest son," he said.

"Perhaps he is taller than rumour measures," she said and winced as pain shot through her, gripping her so tightly that she gasped.

"Your Grace, what is it?" Hatton was on his feet.

"I ate something that disagreed with me, I fear," she gasped out and was doubled up with pain again.

She was vaguely aware of running

feet, of shouting voices, of someone holding her head as she vomited helplessly over the floor, of being lifted and carried, of cold wet cloths on her head and warm ones at her feet, of lights coming and going. The pain gripped her again and flung her against jagged rocks. She had not realized it would hurt so much to die. She was being torn apart and not even Kat was there to put her together again.

She came back down a long tunnel, her head clear, her ribs and throat aching after the strain of constant vomiting. Licking her dry lips she tested her voice,

"Where is Robin?"

"Milord of Leicester has been sitting up with Your Grace these three nights," Doctor Phipps said scoldingly, his bearded face looming into view. "And perhaps Your Grace will cease in future from stuffing yourself with sweetmeats between meals?"

"I was not poisoned?" She felt weakly astonished.

"No, Madam. You ate too much injudiciously of foods that upset you. You must keep to your usual simple diet if you wish to avoid similar attacks in the future."

Promising him meekly she thought that he was wrong. She had not eaten too much, but inside some part of her was being torn apart.

"Your Grace, I am delighted to find you recovered." Thus Walsingham, a few days later, entered the Presence Chamber to bow before her, the usual sheaf of despatches in his hand.

"It was no more than an attack of bile," she said lightly. "What news for me?"

"A letter has been intercepted from the Queen of Scots to Philip of Spain," he told her.

"What an indefatigable letter writer that woman is!" Elizabeth exclaimed, irritated. "What new web is she now weaving?"

"She writes that though for the moment her cause is in eclipse she believes the sun will soon rise for her again, since though her betrothed lord is in prison the Queen of England will not dare to shed such noble blood upon a scaffold."

"You have the letter?" Elizabeth's face had hardened.

"Yes, Madam. It is in cipher with the translation appended." He bowed again, handing it to her.

"The woman is a fool," she said at last, tossing it down. "Such wild and whirling boasts do no kindness to Milord Norfolk. He has written me that he regrets ever having meddled with her."

"He has written to the Queen of Scots telling her he hopes soon to be set at liberty again and to join her," Walsingham said tonelessly.

"By God, those two deserve each other!" she said bitterly.

"Your Grace, one of them must be executed or there will be no peace or safety in the realm," he said. "Milord Burleigh is of the same opinion. There may even be difficulties set in the marriage negotiations with France. Queen Catherine has expressed fears about sending her son into a land where his personal safety might be at risk."

"I am not so certain that I want him to come," she retorted. "As well adopt as wed him when you consider the gap in our ages."

"He is reputed very mature for his years."

"They said that of Anjou," she said restlessly, rising and walking up and down. She had lost weight during her illness and the faint tracery of lines at the corners of her eyes was more pronounced. "Perhaps I was overhasty in declaring that I would never marry a subject. As a woman I have the right to wed where my heart lies."

"But Leicester is married," Walsingham said.

"A widower these — what did you say?" She swung round, her eyes narrowed.

"Milord of Leicester is married," he

said again. His tone was expressionless.

"You lie," she said, equally toneless. "I had not expected that in you, Walsingham. You are allowing your personal dislike to overrule your common sense."

"Your Grace, I have never permitted my personal feelings to affect my judgement," he returned coldly. "He is wed to Lady Sheffield."

"Douglas Sheffield? You have a tale backwards!"

"I check my facts, Madam." He sounded slightly offended. "The young lady was widowed some little time since so I was surprised to hear that she was with child. Further enquiry elicited the information that she was privately married to Milord Leicester. I would not have spoken, but I have no wish to see Your Grace — "

"Make a fool of myself? Where is Leicester?"

"Somewhere about the Court, I believe. Does Your Grace wish — "

"I will see the Earl myself and

untangle what may yet prove to be a slander."

"What of the Duke of Norfolk? I have the new warrant here."

"You are wondrously efficient, Sir Francis," she said bitterly. "Leave it on my desk. I will think about the right course of action to be taken."

As she stepped briskly from the chamber she wished that it was a warrant for Douglas Sheffield's execution that her minister had brought — sly, blonde, light-eyed bitch, being 'consoled' by Robin after the death of an elderly husband for whom she had never cared.

He was at the butts, practising his marksmanship. She paused for a moment to watch, admiring his skill, his heavily handsome frame tensed as he drew back the bowstring, the spring sun bringing out the blue lights in his black hair.

One of his squires evidently brought his attention to the queen's arrival, for he put aside the bow and came to the barrier where she stood.

"Does Your Grace wish to shoot also? We might have a contest, though I fear you might win." He looked as pleased to see her as if he had the conscience of a choirboy.

"Not today, Robin. I am not in a humour for sport," she said, accepting his kiss on her cheek and hand. "Are you aiming well?"

"I am out of practice," he said ruefully.

"Oh, surely not!" She smiled up into his face. "You hit the mark with Douglas Sheffield, did you not?"

"I beg Your Grace's pardon?" He had dropped her hand and the smile on his own lips was somewhat strained.

"Oh, don't seek to cozen me," she said impatiently. "I have known you for too long. Is it true that you are married to her, and if so, how comes it that I must hear the news from others and not from yourself?"

"It is partly true," he said.

"How can a man be partly married?" she said angrily. "Either you are or you are not. Which is it?"

"There was a ceremony," he said reluctantly. "Not an entirely legal one since there were no witnesses, but it satisfied Doug — Lady Sheffield."

"Why did she need to be satisfied?" Elizabeth asked. "No, wait, I will hazard a guess. She is carrying your child so you went through this farce to persuade her the child would be born in wedlock."

"You always see things so clearly, Bess," he began, but she interrupted him furiously.

"Don't Bess me, my lord of Leicester. You got a lady of high estate with child, and were forced into marriage. Don't prate to me of irregularities in the ceremony. If a couple come together before a priest for the purpose of joining in wedlock, then it is not absolutely necessary to have witnesses, and well you know it. You and that — you are married, and without my leave."

"Neither of us need your leave to wed." His broad face had flushed. "We are now both free to marry where we choose."

"But you love me," she said in bewilderment. "You have always loved me."

"And asked you time and time again to be my wife, and time and time again been refused for no good reason that even your Council can fathom. And now you have issued a public notice that you will not wed a subject. That I took to be your final word."

"It is," she said firmly.

"Then I may take a wife who is willing to have me, save that this marriage is no true marriage. It was enacted merely to please the lady."

"I would have thought that you had pleased her sufficiently already," she gibed.

An unwilling grin tugged at the corners of his mouth. The sight of it enraged her further, since it seemed to prove that he was still savouring the pleasure of that young body.

"I will not receive her at Court

again," she said icily, "and you may consider yourself fortunate that I allow you to remain — for the moment."

"To help forward the marriage with Alencon, I suppose? Good God, Bess, he's a pockmarked, dwarfish schoolboy. How could you think of taking him?"

"With my eyes closed and wearing low heels," she retorted, and began to laugh suddenly because, though she was furious with Robin for his perfidy, she need not trouble to rescind the notice she had given and open the door to his perpetual courtship again. Even partly married he was a safe companion for her to enjoy.

"She followed me round everywhere," he complained. "It was always, 'Oh, milord, I am too stupid to deal with this or that matter of business.' She is pretty, that'll I'll grant, but it is a shallow prettiness that will soon fade. I cannot understand how I came to be trapped into such a ceremony."

"Can you not?" She gave him a shrewd glance. "Perhaps you were trying to bring Amy to life again?"

"God forbid!" His grin had been wiped away as she intended. "No, I do believe that I turned to Douglas because I could no longer pretend to myself that there was any chance of your loving me sufficiently to forget your dread of marriage — "

"I do not dread it," she broke in. "Why, since I came to the throne fully half my time has been spent in one proposal after another from so many princes."

Who had all gone off and married other ladies, he thought and might have said, but he was too much in awe of the power she had over his coming to Court to do more than murmur,

"And now you are playing ducks and drakes with Alencon's young heart."

"I hardly think he is overjoyed at the prospect of wedding a woman twice his age," she said wryly. "However so far he has made no such ungallant protest as his brother did. And he may not be as small or as hideous as rumour paints him."

"And I am forgiven? I cannot endure your continued displeasure." He had caught at her hand again, holding it between both his own.

"I am exceedingly angry with you," she pouted. "To rush off like a scolded child and huddle with the foolish Sheffield widow merely because I would not take you. It displays a want of loyalty that cuts me deep. It cuts me very deep, Rob."

"It is Douglas who has cause for complaint," he said. "Every time I kissed her I pretended she was you, and when we bedded I tried to pretend that also was you, surrendering your sweet self at last, but even in fantasy there was no mistaking her for you."

"You still married her," Elizabeth said dryly.

"The stupid girl came to me weeping, telling me that she was carrying my babe. I went through a ceremony to quieten her, no more. She will stay in her house and never come near the Court and I will stay at Court, if it please Your Grace, and never go near her."

"And the child?"

"I'll acknowledge as bastard, no more," he said.

"It will be your first born," she said slyly, and winced inwardly at the sudden look of pride on his face.

He said only, "Any man likes to leave copies of himself."

So there had been love of a sort between him and Douglas, she reflected, raising her hand in farewell and making her way back to her chambers. Whatever else he might say in mitigation of his fault Douglas had known what it was like to give herself completely, what it was like to bear his seed in a swelling belly. Her fists clenching, driving the sharp nails into her palms, she walked on slowly, her head slightly bent.

Burleigh was waiting for her and one glance at his face told her he had been talking to Walsingham.

"I have been scolding Milord Leicester," she said, entering gaily. "He has gotten that Douglas Sheffield with child too late for her to foist it on her late husband. Is he not beyond redemption, Cecil?"

"There was some talk of a marriage," he said cautiously.

"A ceremony to satisfy convention, no more," she said. "It keeps the lady quiet and it is also in my best interests. Now he will never be able to importunate me again to be his wife, when he has one already. It sets me free to pursue the match with Alencon."

"If that is what Your Grace wishes," he said, still cautious.

"It is precisely what I want," she said. "Write again to Queen Catherine and tell her that I would have an exact description of her son's want of complexion. Exact."

"Yes, Your Grace."

"And make sure — what's this?" Reaching her desk she looked down at the parchment there.

"The death warrant for the Duke of Norfolk," Burleigh said without emphasis.

"Oh." She sat down, reaching for her pen, dipping it neatly into the ink. Over her shoulder, still lightly, she said,

"I wish I could deal so easily with all traitors."

6

THE old palace of Westminster had seldom looked more splendid, with the flags of England and France flying together from the turrets and thousands of candles illuminating the great halls and the grounds that stretched to the abbey.

The Duke of Montmorency and the Ambassador, La Motte, had been cheered through the streets by crowds who took this treaty to set the seal on the betrothal between their queen and Alencon. True, he was little more than a boy, but boys were lusty and their Bess deserved a lusty lad. It was generally agreed that the prince ought to have come himself to be looked over as it were, but there were whispers that Leicester had spoken out against it. He was still dabbling his fingers in the queen's private affairs as if he hadn't just seduced (the lady swore married) Lady Sheffield. She was certainly not with her new bridegroom who rode in his accustomed place next to the queen, his plumed hat concealing the slight thinning of his dark hair, his carriage as arrogant as if he had been born to the purple.

Elizabeth overshadowed even the most splendidly clad of her retinue, her skirts of white satin spangled with golden suns and silver moons, the tight bodice corseted in deep purple, the huge puffed sleeves cuffed in white lace to match the high pleated ruff that closed tightly about her throat with the flesh beneath glinting with ropes of diamonds and pearls. Her small crown was set with the same gems and, in the light of the torches and the candles, she was less a woman than a glittering goddess risen to compensate the people for the loss of the Holy Virgin to whom they were now told it was wrong to pray.

"Madam, you diminish the sun,"

La Motte complimented her as she accepted his hand to step down from her litter.

"Mr Ambassador, you have not lost your silver tongue," she said archly. "I hope that your duke of Alencon has as flattering a one."

"No, he does not flatter," La Motte said promptly. "Indeed he speaks very little these days. He spends hours at a time gazing at your portrait and wishing that he were in possession of the original."

"Is he so plain of countenance that he can hope for nothing better than a bride twice his age?" she enquired.

"In appearance he is greatly improved," the ambassador assured her. "Oh, his skin was sadly marked by the smallpox but he has been applying a new lotion which is having a marvellous effect."

"Perhaps I will try it myself," Elizabeth said.

"Your complexion needs no lotions," he said.

It was not mere compliment. Her

skin, under its light coating of paint, was as fair and delicate as when she had been a girl. There was now a faint crepiness at her throat and her eyelids and her teeth were dull, but she had retained her looks to a remarkable degree.

"Let us hope that Alencon sees with your partial eyes," she said, pleased by his remark. She had always had a personal liking for the ambassador though she trusted him not at all. He was far more amusing than the powerfully built Montmorency at her other side who seemed incapable of stringing two coherent sentences together without blushing.

The banquet had been laid in Westminster Hall, the long tables set upon the high dais, the musicians already strumming their instruments softly in the gallery. The display of gold plate, crystal goblets and ivory-handled cutlery would dazzle even the sophisticated guests, and make them realize anew that in marrying the Queen of England Alencon would be entering into a rich inheritance.

"The decanters are surely Venetian, Your Grace," La Motte said, making as usual the very comment designed to please.

"Francis Drake presented them as a New Year gift," Elizabeth said coyly.

"The pirate," Montmorency commented, somewhat sourly.

"He is a fine captain," she demurred, "and trades for me. I would not countenance piracy."

"Yet it is truly amazing how often the contents of Spanish trading ships end up in the ports of England," La Motte said, his mouth twitching.

"The Spanish are often very careless with their cargoes," she answered, bright-eyed.

"If this alliance with our two countries holds strong — " Montmorency began.

"If?" Elizabeth gave him a sharp look. "I like not your 'ifs', sir."

"Treaties have been broken before," he insisted.

"Never by England," she said proudly, "save when it was absolutely necessary."

"We are all praying that this treaty will be crowned by Your Grace's nuptials," La Motte said.

"We will discuss the precise terms tomorrow," she told him. "This evening is for gaiety."

The food echoed that intention. The finest ducks had been shot and killed, coney and hare pies vied with oyster patties, with great bowls of vegetables simmered in honey and ginger, and each course was followed by subtleties depicting in spun sugar and jelly and marzipan figures from both French and English history. Each dish was paraded about the table and then applauded before being served on bended knee.

The queen ate little, toying with each dish before it was removed, sipping from the same goblet of wine. When she was happy, as she was tonight, she had small appetite. Only when the old nightmare visited her or some anxiety proved insoluble did she cram sweetmeats into her mouth, seeking to assuage the terrible hunger that gripped her.

She glanced down the long table, her eyes flicking over the faces ranged along it. Here were her most trusted councillors — Burleigh, Walsingham, Hatton, Heneage, Arundel, Sussex and her one true love, Robin, though he was not carrying his years as well as she did. He had gained a trifle too much weight and his hair was beginning to recede, but he was still handsome and vigorous. There were younger members of her Court here too — Philip Sidney, son of the Lord Deputy of Ireland who was already writing graceful verse and John Harrington, her own godson, whose father had served Tom Seymour so faithfully. Her ladies she viewed with a stricter eye, alert for any conduct on their part that might tell against her own reputation. It was fortunate that both Kat Ashley and Blanche Parry kept a tight rein on their high spirits, though there were also times when, hearing the laughter issuing from the maidens' quarters when their duties were done she envied their careless high spirits. Tonight they sat demurely, their gowns charming but never detracting from the finery of their royal mistress. A little further down the table, her plump hands reaching for the dainties, her own cousin, Lady Lennox, daughter of her aunt, Margaret Tudor, merited a long, considering look.

Margaret Tudor had married twice, giving her first husband, the king of Scotland, the boy who would father Mary Stuart. Meg was her daughter by her second marriage and had herself borne two sons. Darnley the elder had wed his cousin, Mary of Scots, and been murdered with what was generally believed to have been his wife's connivance, and the younger, Charles, was now at the family seat in Yorkshire. Meg Lennox came seldom to Court, and when she did she made it clear that in her opinion the Scottish side of the family was infinitely superior to the child of a Boleyn.

Elizabeth preferred her Howard cousins who were lively and witty, and had made not the least attempt to speak on behalf of their relative, the Duke of Norfolk.

"Something displeases Your Grace?" La Motte said, seeing her face momentarily darken.

"Nothing." She smiled at him, raising her goblet slightly. "I was just thinking that as welcome as your company is I long to see the Duke of Alencon at my table."

"Amen to that," he added. "May I venture to say that we in France will not be content until he is also in your bedchamber as your affianced husband?"

"You must spare my blushes, sir," she said coyly, her long eyes laughing. "I am a spinster lady."

The banquet was drawing to its end. A knight in armour rode into the great hall, thudding with his long staff upon the flagstones as he cried,

"Great Majesty of England, two companies of brave men seek your permission to joust."

"A tournament by candlelight!" She clapped her hands, feigning surprise. "By all means let us have jousting. Come, my lords."

Sweeping ahead of her courtiers into the gardens, now transformed into a wonderland with lanterns strung along the water's edge, and guards holding flambeaux to illuminate the lists and the tiers of seats for the spectators, she glided like a shimmering moth over the grass. Jousting had always excited her as did hunting and the sports of bear and bull baiting. They satisfied something in her nature that was savage and primitive, buried beneath the silks and satins of courtly etiquette.

In her ear Leicester whispered, "How long will you flatter these Frenchmen, my Bess?"

"Behave yourself!" She tapped him sharply on the arm, turning smilingly to her guests.

The tournament was more of a mêlée since the combatants, being clad in white and pale blue, had the colours of their cloaks drained by the moon so that more than once there were shouts of indignation as two knights found themselves wrestling together though both were on the same team. It only added to the general merriment which grew and swelled and echoed across the dark waters of the Thames now pinpointed by a thousand dancing lights. Burleigh whose gout was not improved by this exposure to the night air sighed inwardly and hoped that the contest would soon end. It did so just before dawn with no more damage than a couple of broken legs and a concussion sustained by one of the older knights who had been advised not to compete in the first place and so received scant sympathy.

"It is a tie," Elizabeth announced.

There was a burst of cheering from the spectators, some of the enthusiasm due more to the tournament having ended than out of compliment for the skills of the contestants. Leicester, rubbing the stubble on his chin and stifling a yawn, glanced at Elizabeth who looked as crisp and fresh as if she had spent the whole night sleeping. She had reserves of energy on which she could draw without diminishing them.

"We shall meet at ten," she informed her visitors, "and talk more of this marriage. There are many matters to be discussed."

At ten she was waiting for them, her gown exchanged for a looser robe of greeny blue, its farthingale smaller, its ruff less exaggerated. She looked cool and sweet, her eyelids not even darkened after a night without sleep. Both La Motte and Montmorency looked weary.

"I have been examining the portrait of the duke which Queen Catherine was so kind as to send me," she began without preamble. "He does seem to have rather a large nose."

"It is indeed somewhat large," La

Motte admitted.

"And his height is — ?"

"A little lower than Your Majesty," Montmorency said.

"I am five feet seven inches. How high does he stand?"

"Five feet three inches," La Motte said, with a gesture of resignation. "He does frequently wear blocked heels."

"Four inches difference." She was silent, considering. "And pockmarked too."

"The lotion is improving that," La Motte assured her. "What you cannot see in any portrait is the grace of his carriage or the charm of his voice. Though any initial sight of him shall work to his disadvantage he improves vastly on further acquaintance. I will grant you he is not as handsome as his elder brother."

Elizabeth made a little gesture as if she were brushing a fly away with her hand. The Duke of Anjou had recently been elected as King of Poland and was rumoured to have fallen in love at last with a member of the opposite sex, a princess of Lorraine.

"There is also the matter of his religion," she was continuing. "As you know it was impossible for me to accept Milord of Anjou because he insisted on observing the Catholic mass here and by law that is forbidden."

"Is that law so strictly enforced?" Montmorency asked.

"The Catholics pay recusancy fines," she told him. "It would hardly do for the king to have to pay such fines."

"The duke will not insist on practising his religion," La Motte assured her.

"I would not like to think that he had no religion at all," she objected.

"He is," said the ambassador, "of a tolerant persuasion."

"We would need to be assured of his own safety in this realm," Montmorency said bluntly.

"Of that he may be fully assured. This match is desired by my people."

"There is no further danger of rebellion then?"

"My cousin of Norfolk paid the penalty." Her face had hardened.

"But the Queen of Scots is still held captive in the north," Montmorency said.

"She is held pending an enquiry into the murder of her husband."

"Would it not relieve Your Grace of a burden if she were allowed to cross into France?"

The heavy white lids were lowered over the sea-coloured eyes. With Mary in France Catherine de Medici could pull the strings in England, making both Elizabeth and her son dance to her tune under threat of supporting the Stuart claim.

"Let us leave Mary where she is," she said at last. "Tell me more of Alencon's tastes. Does he like to hunt? To dance?"

"He longs to do both with Your Grace," La Motte told her. "He has sent a private gift, a token he wishes you to accept for his sake."

"A present?" Her eyes had brightened.

La Motte bowed, handing her a small velvet covered box. Opening it she took out a brooch, fashioned from an emerald in the shape of a frog.

"Your Grace knows the old fairy tale?" La Motte spoke somewhat hurriedly, seeing the frown on her face. "The prince was turned by evil enchantment into a frog until the beautiful princess kissed him and so restored him to his own shape again."

"A charming conceit!" The frown had faded. "So he designates himself the frog prince, does he? And mine is the kiss that will restore him to his true shape? Well, well, we shall see."

But when the Court set out on summer progress to Warwick the next day La Motte noticed with some satisfaction that the plumed riding hat of the queen was pinned up at one side with the emerald frog.

These progresses were becoming a regular annual event instead of the occasional excursions they had been in her father's reign. King Harry had made progresses when he had wished to terrify some region into submission. His daughter regarded them as an opportunity to let her people catch a glimpse of their powerful and amiable queen. She had worked out her route and intimated which households she would be honouring with a visit during the spring. That gave the chance to prepare for her coming and, where necessary, to land themselves deeply in debt in their efforts to entertain her retinue adequately. While she was absent her various palaces could be cleaned and rid of vermin and she herself could enjoy, as many of her courtiers did not, long hours on horseback riding in glittering procession through the leafy lanes.

This summer her progress was into Warwickshire. She would spend a night at the manor of Sir George Pomfret and then move into Warwick Castle, a pleasant prospect since she was fond of both Earl and Countess. Meanwhile the long, winding cumbersome procession was forming, with the enormous trunks containing her garments and the garments of her courtiers lashed to the carts that lumbered ahead, with the household menials following at a run on foot or, if their position warranted it, mounted on ponies. Behind them marched and rode the guards, their spears glinting, their helmets pulled low, the banners of the attendant nobles flashing scarlet, azure, gold, emerald, peacock and silver. The Court proper brought up the rear, most of them riding though a few of the very old clung to the swaying litters.

La Motte could have dispensed with his own invitation to form part of this glittering cavalcade. He found the queen's passion for junketing about the southern counties of her realm inconvenient and time wasting and her desire to be seen by her subjects and to allow her subjects to see her quite incomprehensible. The French monarchs stayed in their castles save for hunting trips which struck him as a much more sensible way of conducting affairs. He envied Montmorency who had returned to Paris to continue the preliminary negotiations.

Elizabeth however was oblivious to his discomfort and weariness as she pointed with her whip at various features of the landscape.

"This is excellent grazing land. However one must find the right balance between sheep and cattle. Sheep will denude pasture land very swiftly which is excellent for the wool trade, but unfortunate for our agriculture. We are providing some protection by enclosing many more farms to keep the sheep out and the grain in. At least serfdom is abolished. The tenant farmers are their own masters."

It was not entirely correct since the tenants were too often dependent on the whim of an absentee landlord, and the Poor Laws were harsh equating poverty with idleness and making honest men down on their luck into outlaws and beggars, but at least the great majority of the people appeared well fed and contented with their lot.

"My great grandsire, Henry the Seventh, saw when he came to the throne that prosperity is the eldest daughter of trade," she said. "He encouraged initiative wherever he found it."

She was more like him than her splendidly barbaric father, the ambassador thought, despite her elaborate dress and moonlight tournaments. Such entertainments were as carefully calculated as the childlike delight she displayed now as she pointed out the prosperity of her realm.

Approaching the walls of Warwick she checked her mount, nodding towards the group of robed dignitaries waiting by the ancient gate.

"The Mayor and Town Council will greet us now and offer a gift. One hopes it will be worth taking," she said. "The harvest was poor last year and many of the sheep caught the murrain, so one must not expect too much. Come, sir, and we shall test how my subjects love me."

The mayor, robed in scarlet, was on his knees offering the mace in token of submission. Elizabeth touched it with a long shapely hand, and reined in her horse to listen to the long address of welcome uttered in dog Latin by the perspiring worthy. From the look on her face she might never have heard better.

"Such a welcome no monarch ever enjoyed before." She answered in English, the tedious speech having finally trailed to a lame conclusion. "Your words were most fair, sir. Most affecting."

"If you please, Your Grace, twas composed by our Recorder, Master Aglionby, and he was too much in awe indeed to mouth them," the mayor confessed.

"Not afraid of his queen surely?" She looked about her and raised her voice. "Mr Recorder, we pray you to step forward."

An extremely short man, quivering with nerves from head to foot, was pushed forward by his companions.

"Come hither, little Master Recorder," she invited. "So you are nervous at the prospect of meeting me. I swear to you that I was very nervous at the thought of meeting one who could put my own Latin to shame with such eloquence. We will comfort each other with a hearty English handshake for I am mere English like yourself."

Leaning from the saddle, she shook the little man's hand.

"Now he will not wash for a month," Hatton whispered.

"Your G-grace," the Recorder stammered, "we have a gift for Your Grace."

"Oh, but this was not expected." She clasped her hands and shook her head playfully in Leicester's direction. "You promised me that there would be no gifts this year, for God forbid that any town should be further impoverished merely because I choose to visit it."

"It is only twenty pounds, Your Grace," the mayor said blushingly.

"Twenty pounds from this town is worth ten times its weight in gold," she declared. "I am deeply moved by this proof of your love and generosity. The gift will be put to good use, I promise you. God bless you all."

They crowded about to kiss her hand, their faces shining with as much gratitude as if they had been the ones to receive the twenty pounds.

"Your monarch has the common touch," La Motte said, genuinely impressed.

"Of course," Burleigh said, easing himself briefly in the saddle and wishing he had elected to travel by litter. "She is England incarnate and we are all reflected in her face."

It was a warm and scented summer, the bees busy in the hearts of the blossoms, the queen on horseback from dawn to dusk. The woods rang with the sounds of crashing hoofs, barking dogs, the hiss of arrows, the cries of 'View Halloo' as the quarry was sighted and tracked. In the evenings there were long leisurely suppers after which the queen danced or yielded to persuasion and swept her long fingers across the strings of her lute. And always there was one of the Council to draw the ambassador's attention to the prosperity that surrounded their queen, the affectionate respect with which she was regarded, the rich heritage into which Alencon would enter if the treaty held.

They established themselves in the great castle of Warwick, spilling out into the surrounding manors. Leicester's own mansion of Kenilworth was not far distant, and on occasion when they rode too far in the forest they broke their journey within the ivy clad walls where wine and comfits were provided by his own servants.

It was during the second week of their progress that despatches arrived from France that sent Milord Burleigh hurrying to the queen, his mild face so black that she stared at it in alarm.

"For God's sake, Cecil, what ails you?"

"The most evil news that man can conceive," he said.

"Alencon is dead!" It was the first thing that came into her head.

"No, Your Grace but two thousand others are." His usual urbanity had deserted him.

"Be plain with me," she commanded.

"Two nights ago on the day of Saint Bartholomew," he said, wiping sweat from his brow, "the Protestants of Paris were massacred by order of the King of France."

"It isn't possible." Her own voice was hushed in horror.

"Despatches from our own ambassador," Burleigh said. "The tocsin was sounded as a prearranged signal and the troops of King Charles fell upon every Protestant, every Huguenot that dwelt within the city walls. Men, women and children were butchered, tossed on bayonets, torn limb from limb, gutted like slain deer. It does not bear the thinking about."

"What of the Huguenot leaders? Admiral Coligny? The Prince of Navarre?"

"Navarre had been invited to a reception in the palace but for some reason neglected to arrive. Perhaps he had private warning. Coligny was wounded and taken prisoner. Some of the Catholic citizens tried to shelter their Protestant friends and were dragged out and killed for their pains. It was done on the personal orders of King Charles."

"And I considered him once as a possible husband," she cried bitterly. "Was it simply for religious reasons this outrage was performed? I cannot believe so."

"Queen Catherine needs money and land in which the Protestants, being hard working and for the most part thrifty, are well supplied," he told her. "Oh, there is some tale of plots suspected but nobody takes heed of that falsehood."

She was silent for a long while, her eyes lowered. In her mind the fires of Smithfield flamed skywards again as they had in her sister's reign. The law of De Heretico Comurendo was still technically in force in England, but since she had ascended the throne only two Anabaptists who had insisted on denying the Anglican Canon loudly in public over and over had been burned, and it was generally felt they had chosen martyrdom. This massacre of two thousand innocent people who had never harmed their neighbours or thrust their opinions down other throats was on a scale that horrified her and would turn the most of England against the new alliance with France.

"Where is La Motte?" she asked.

"I left him perusing the despatches. He is as shocked as we are."

"Request him to wait upon us tomorrow. Have heralds sent to cry the news in our cities, and order the Court and Commons into mourning for a month," she instructed.

When La Motte entered the royal presence on the following day it was to be greeted by a silent, sable-clad Court and a queen whose own dress was of black satin against which her face and hands glowed eerily white.

"Mr Ambassador." She stepped towards him, not offering her hand. "This news from France strikes us to the heart," she said. "I will pay you the compliment of believing that you were ignorant of these plans."

"Your Grace," he said truthfully, "I had no inkling that such action was intended. The plans were kept most secret."

"What possible justification can there be for such an act?" She had moved aside with him to an embrasure where stood a solitary chair. She seated herself on this, obliging him to drop to his knee.

"In my own letter from His Majesty,"

he began stumblingly, "there is word of plots against the lives of himself and the Queen Mother. He writes that it was necessary to take such steps for his own security."

"Indeed?" Her voice was softly sarcastic. "Yes, I can see how threatening the Huguenot babes must have seemed as they had their heads dashed against the walls or were spitted like small chickens on the spears of His most Catholic Majesty's guards."

"Madam, I am as shocked as yourself," he said unhappily, "and can offer no explanation."

"If there have in truth been plots against your master then those suspected should have been arrested and not butchered without trial. I cannot believe for one instant in so feeble an excuse for what every country will rightly regard as wholesale murder."

"Your Grace, I have no further explanation until I hear again from France," La Motte said unhappily.

"You do understand that all future

discussions concerning my betrothal to the Duke of Alencon must be suspended?"

"Your Grace, the duke was not even in Paris when the — unfortunate accident occurred," he assured her.

"I am glad to hear it." She bit her lip, considering. Or pretending to consider, La Motte guessed, knowing her habits.

"This betrothal is a matter very near to my own heart," he said.

"I cannot think of it now with the horror of this massacre fresh in my mind," she said at last. "I do not hold you personally responsible, of course, for the blood lusts of your king — yes, blood lusts, sir! I will not call it less, not for any excuse in the world. You may leave us for the time while we consult with our Council."

Knowing that any protest would only anger her more he withdrew, watched by the silent Court. Her Council were certainly in no doubt as to the appropriate action to be taken.

183

"Bring the Queen of Scots to trial and execute her," Burleigh said flatly.

"Before or after the verdict?" Elizabeth enquired.

"Your Grace, what difference does it make? She has encouraged plots against your life and your throne. Were such plots to succeed it would be the Protestants of England who would face death."

"My cousin of Scots is no fanatic."

"But if her freedom is gained she will take another husband from one of the Papist states and it is he who will rule for she is always ruled by the man in her life," Walsingham urged.

"I will execute nobody." She banged her fist on the table, her voice quiet and cold. "I will not stain my hands with the blood of a sister sovereign. I will not join that bloodstained crew across the Channel who hide their greed for property under pretence of feared treasons. Sir Francis, I am sending you into France as my ambassador extraordinary to make stringent enquiry into this sorry affair."

"What of the marriage negotiations with Alencon?" Sussex asked. "Are they now cancelled?"

"Postponed." Her fingers crossed the frog brooch on her dress. "Postponed for the moment."

7

SHE had not imagined when she spoke those words that the negotiations would be postponed for two long years. The revulsion felt throughout England at the measure on Saint Bartholomew's day had rendered any talk of a Catholic marriage anathema to her subjects.

Her own councillors had argued long and hard for the trial of the Queen of Scots to begin, but she had steadfastly refused. There was no logical reason why she should not put Mary on trial but deep within herself she felt that it established a dangerous precedent.

Now two years later Charles of France was dead and his brother, Anjou, was crowned king with his little princess of Lorraine at his side.

"And Alencon now is made Duke of Anjou in his stead," she observed to Burleigh. "Faith, 'tis like a ladder with the ones at the top vanishing into eternity. Do you think the soul of the French king was greeted by those he had sent there ahead of their due date?"

"For his soul's sake I hope not," he answered.

"Well, it's no matter. It is a Henry who sits upon the throne now, propped up by his bitch mother, and Alencon is become Anjou. Has he grown, I wonder?"

"In wisdom perhaps," Burleigh said.

"And he wishes to reopen the negotiations. He is still much younger than I am, Cecil."

"I've told Your Grace before that cannot be altered," he said patiently. "The mood of the country has softened in the time since the massacre. Provided there be adequate safeguards to protect both your Catholic and Protestant subjects the marriage will be welcomed."

"Next month," she said, "I celebrate my forty-first year. If I am to have children then we must not waste too much time."

"Your Grace's health is good?" he asked delicately.

"The hymen has stretched sufficiently due to the excessive riding Your Grace enjoys to make full penetration more likely," her physician had told her. "There is no physical bar to your marrying and conceiving as far as I can tell, Your Grace."

"My health is splendid," she answered Burleigh now, "and I am anxious to bear children. The country must have heirs of my body. And we need that French alliance still though I was angry to hear from Walsingham that a mockery of my Court was staged for the amusement of the Medici woman."

"The dwarfs," Burleigh said with a resigned air.

"Twisted freaks dressed up as my lord father and his wives and as myself and Leicester," she said white-faced. "A monstrous insult to me and my crown. And Walsingham was forced to sit through it and endure it."

"An apology has been received," he told her.

"Oh?" She tilted her head expectantly.

"The Queen Mother sends to say that the entertainment was not understood by Sir Francis in the spirit it was intended. The dwarfs were not grotesque but very pretty and well formed. She is devastated that the masque should have displeased. Do we accept the excuse?"

"Of course." Elizabeth shrugged. "Have a letter drafted thanking dear Queen Catherine for her friendly explanation and tell her how much I wish she would send me her pretty little midgets so that I could reward them as they deserve."

"I think she will not send them," Burleigh said, smothering a smile.

"I think that you are right," Elizabeth said. "I swear I would make them sing another tune. So, we must grit our teeth and smile and hope that Alencon is better than the rest of his benighted clan."

"He is disliked by his brother," Burleigh said.

"Then there's hope for him. Perhaps we can mould him between us into a husband fit for me?"

"If you want my frank opinion," he said, "there is no man on earth who could ever match your qualities, but with Alencon at least we get the treaty with France renewed and some protection against the threats of Spain."

"Philip has been threatening me ever since he was wed to my poor sister," Elizabeth grinned.

"He demands that you either return to the true faith, as he terms it, or set Mary Stuart free," Burleigh said.

"I am not interested in the demands of the King of Spain." The amusement had vanished from her face. "You will reopen the negotiations with France."

"Yes, Your Grace." He made some rapid notes on the pad he was holding, then looked up again.

"Is there anything more?"

Outside the leaves were beginning

to turn from green to scarlet, the roses dropping their petals, the wind autumn scented. It had been a long hot summer but now she craved the start of winter.

"Unfortunately there is," he said.

"What?" She swung round from the oriel window through which she had been gazing.

"There has been a wedding," Burleigh said.

"Whose?"

"Lord Charles Lennox to Mistress Elizabeth Cavendish," he said.

"Cousin Meg's boy has married Shrewsbury's stepdaughter?" She gaped at him in astonishment.

"It seems so," he said.

"How dare they? How came it about? Where is my cousin of Lennox?" She had strode to the bell and was tugging the rope furiously.

"Your Grace, I would advise — "

"Be quiet, Cecil. This is a family matter." She addressed the servant who had hurried in.

"Tell the Countess of Lennox to come here immediately. Immediately!"

"Strictly speaking the Countess Margaret has broken no law," her minister said.

"Have you forgotten that she was Darnley's mother?" Elizabeth said angrily. "Have you forgotten that the mother of Elizabeth Cavendish is wife to the man in whose keeping I have confided the Queen of Scots? Have you forgotten that the Lennoxes stand after Mary Stuart and her son in the line of succession? Why do my relatives insist on making marriages that will displease me. First the Grey girls — " She referred to the sisters of Lady Jane, both of whom had made imprudent matches and received life imprisonment in the Tower for their pains. The widower of Katherine Grey had been reinstated in his titles and made a second marriage with her cousin on the Boleyn side, such an alliance being no threat to her own position, but the political implications of any courtly love affair were never far from her mind.

The Countess came at once though it was too slowly for the queen whose fingers were ripping at the handkerchief she carried.

"Your Grace sent for me?" She curtsied, her plump figure wobbling slightly. The daughter of the queen's aunt, Margaret Tudor, Meg Lennox had inherited the Tudor tendency to put on weight. She had been a handsome, arrogant girl and now she was a formidable matron, in her forties but with her flaming red hair and plump features seeming younger.

"I understand that I have to wish you joy," Elizabeth said, dangerously sweet.

"Your Grace?"

"Don't fence with me, cousin," Elizabeth said sharply. "Your foil is blunted. You have married your son to Shrewsbury's girl."

"Yes, Your Grace." The answer came promptly.

"You did not see fit to inform anyone

of it? To ask permission?"

"I was not aware that permission needed to be sought," Meg said. "I cannot treat my son like a child now that he is of age."

"How did he meet Elizabeth Cavendish?" Elizabeth demanded.

"It was the fortunes of Cupid, Your Grace," Meg said. Her rather prominent blue eyes were slyly mocking. "The Countess of Shrewsbury was kind enough to invite me to stay with her at Chatsworth — "

"Where the Queen of Scots has recently been moved," Elizabeth interrupted. "Since when do my courtiers rush up to pay their respects in that quarter?"

"The Queen of Scots was wed to my late son," Meg said boldly. "I have small cause to love her since she has never been cleared of complicity in his most foul murder. I did not pay her any honour."

"By God, you had better not!" The queen took several turns about the room, trying to calm herself. "So you visited the Shrewsburys. Go on."

"My son was taken ill with the measles during the day we spent there," Meg said, and smirked.

"So he had perforce to remain until the infection had passed. No, don't trouble to explain. I see it very clearly, as clearly as if you had drawn me a portrait. Elizabeth Cavendish had no recourse but to sit with him while he recovered, and the pretty pair fell so deeply in love that neither you nor the Shrewsburys could refuse to let them wed. Go to, you must take me for a fool! It was plotted between you. The Shrewsburys strive to rise in the world very high and you seek to engender a rival line."

"No, Your Grace." For the first time a hint of unease appeared in her cousin's face. "We had no such thought. I would remind Your Grace however that Charles is fourth in the direct line of — "

"It is not wise," Elizabeth said, "to

boast of your bloodline, my lady. My father disinherited the descendants of his sister, Margaret of Scotland, because he liked not her greed or her morals. Have a care that I do not follow his example. Your son is of the blood royal as you keep reminding me, and therefore his marriage is an affair of state. You should have asked for my consent. You and the Shrewsburys think yourself monarchs of Yorkshire, but you will learn that London has a long arm. Guards!"

In every palace there were always guards within earshot, trained to come, to obey without question. As they entered she had the pleasure of seeing her cousin's high colour fade to a sickly white.

"Since you are so fond of paying visits," she said, "you may prepare to pay a lengthy visit to the Tower. Your partner in crime, Bess Shrewsbury, will speedily join you there. Not one word!"

With grudging admiration she saw the other gather up the rags of her dignity, incline her vivid head and walk away, straight backed, the guards following.

"She has not committed any crime, you know," Burleigh said calmly, "save that of imprudence."

"She and her son are both, as she so kindly reminded me, in the direct bloodline. His wife should have been my own choice."

"I had not realized that Your Grace was so eager for your relatives to marry," Burleigh murmured.

She snapped him a furious look and then began unexpectedly to giggle.

"You are right, my old friend," she said. "I have no wish to sit upon the throne round which claimants snarl and clamour for recognition. My grandfather was wise, for he beggared the nobility and executed the last of the Plantagenets."

"He also sired four children," Burleigh reminded her.

"An example I will follow as soon as my marriage to Alencon — who is now Anjou — is arranged. I cannot bear children until I am wed."

"What is to be done with the Countess of Lennox?" he enquired.

"Has she really committed no crime?"

"She was ill-mannered not to inform you of the betrothal, but that is no crime."

"But not even to inform me," Elizabeth argued, "can surely be construed as impertinence?"

"Grave impertinence, Your Grace."

"Then she and the Countess of Shrewsbury can kick their heels in the Tower for a few months. I've small doubt their respective spouses will be delighted, since I hear they are both scolds. And Shrewsbury shall pay a fine."

"And the young couple?" There was a trace of anxiety in his face.

"Let them enjoy their honeymoon in Yorkshire and not show their faces at my Court," she said after a brief hesitation. "My own betrothal is so near that I am disposed to mercy. Will you hunt with us tomorrow?"

"I have too much business, Your Grace." He rose somewhat stiffly.

"Work tonight and ride tomorrow."

"Madam, I lack your energy," he said ruefully.

"Poor Cecil, I work you hard, don't I?" In brief compunction she put her hand on his arm.

"I thrive on it," he assured her.

"Of all my councillors I could least spare you," she told him. "Sometimes I regret the need to take any husband for you and I work well together."

"I do not believe that your marriage will alter that," he said.

"I shall not allow my marriage to alter anything," she said. "I saw my sister, Mary, tie herself into knots to please Spanish Philip, and he despised her for it. Every cruelty that was introduced during her reign was at his behest, and yet she was blamed and died hated by the people she longed to serve. I'll never permit that to happen for me."

"If Your Grace means to be both

master and mistress then it was wise not to accept Milord Leicester," he approved.

"Oh, I learned wisdom in childhood," she said wryly. "Douglas Sheffield had a son. Did you know?"

"Leicester claims that the child is bastard, that his marriage to Lady Sheffield is invalid."

"Of course." She curved her lips into a tight little smile, making a flicking motion with her fingers as if she were ridding herself of an unimportant nuisance.

"I will attend to the correspondence, Madam." His smile was reassuring.

"I fully intend to take the French boy, you know?" She detained him for an instant. "I can feel the years running through my life like sand in an hour-glass."

"There is still time, Your Grace."

Bowing, he withdrew. She gazed after him thoughtfully, seeing the limp and the grey hair like some presage of her own future.

"Is it true?" Kat Ashley had entered unceremoniously, her face flushed with indignation.

"Is what true?"

"That Milady Lennox has matched her son with the Cavendish girl and both mothers are ordered to the Tower?"

"You think I am too harsh?"

"Too gentle more like," Kat said decidedly. "You let them take advantage of your good nature, lovie. I have warned you a thousand times that the Lennoxes are greedy, hands held out for what was never theirs in the first place. The pair of them want ducking."

"What a pity you are not on my Privy Council," Elizabeth murmured.

The governess snorted to indicate that such an opinion went without saying.

"I am not separating the couple," Elizabeth went on. "Do you think that too kindly in me?"

"Is she with child?" Kat asked.

"I don't think so. The two were coaxed into love by the combined efforts of their two mamas for the twin reasons of money which the Shrewsburys have and high rank which the Lennoxes can supply. I shall leave them be, provided they stay away from my Court. Pray let us talk of something more pleasurable. I am sick and tired of my relatives."

"There is a relative of my own I'd have you meet," Kat said.

"Who?" Elizabeth looked questioning.

"A half-brother of Sir Humphrey Gilbert's who is, as you know, cousin to my late husband. His name is Raleigh, Walter Raleigh."

"Another time, Kat. I have too much on my mind now. The courtiers already here give me quite sufficient trouble without my increasing their numbers," Elizabeth said irritably. "Philip Sidney insulted Oxford yesterday. Oh, the puppy richly deserved to be taken down but not by one of inferior rank. I have sent young Philip to cool his temper at his father's house for a few weeks until he learns more discretion. Sometimes those who surround me remind me of curs snarling over a bone."

Her irritability exploded into mirth and she clapped Kat on the shoulder as she went from the room.

As she had expected her ladies were huddled together whispering the latest news. She heard a stifled giggle or two and guessed that her cousin's incarceration would meet with scant sympathy. Meg Lennox was not a popular figure. Her arrogance and the single-minded greed with which she pursued her objectives had won her few friends, and though as the mother of the murdered Darnley she had been accorded a measure of pity it was generally agreed that the Queen of Scots' husband had been a contemptible youth when he was alive anyway.

"Have you nothing with which to occupy yourselves?" she said, raising her voice sharply.

"Your Grace, is it true that the Countess of Lennox is sent to the Tower?" one of the bolder asked.

"Did you wish to join her there?" Elizabeth enquired sweetly. "It can be arranged."

"No, Madam." The girl drew back, her face paling.

"Then find something to do." She looked about the ring of young, fresh faces and said, her own face darkening. "From all reports you spend your time in giggling and gossiping. Sir Matthew Arundel has complained to me that your chatter prevents him from sleeping at nights."

"His room is next to our dormitory, Your Grace, and he retires very early," Mary Scudamore said. "He's an old grouch."

"That will do." Elizabeth hastily stifled a grin. "Sir Matthew is an elderly and respected gentleman and deserves our respect. Keep your mirth within bounds."

They were scattering to their

embroidery frames with expressions of virtue pinned to their faces. She calculated that the decorum would last until some good-looking court gallant came sauntering by. For the moment they sat demurely, eyes lowered under her stern regard.

Their morals were her responsibility, she reflected. Their parents had sent them to Court so that their marital prospects would be improved. When one girl allowed herself to be seduced it reflected on her. Too many believed that she had already leaped the pale with Leicester, so it was important for her to maintain strict discipline. For now they were occupied. Her satisfaction pierced by a curious regret, she continued on her way to the Council Chamber. The order committing the two meddlesome women would have to be drawn up and signed.

She had almost reached the end of the corridor, shadowed now by the going down of the sun, when a figure emerged from one of the anterooms that abutted it, and came towards her, in figure, colouring and gait so like herself that a shiver of superstitious horror thrilled along her nerves and she stopped dead though the other continued to approach.

"Your Grace, I didn't see you in the gloom." The figure that was almost the twin of her own paused with an exaggerated little start.

"I did not know you were at Court, cousin," Elizabeth said.

Lettice Knollys was the daughter of Mary Boleyn who had pleasured King Harry before he saw her sister, Anne. She had been wed to the Earl of Essex and seldom came to London. Elizabeth had forgotten how alike they were, of similar height and shape with the same pale skins and red-gold hair. Lettice's eyes were brown however, her features thinner than the queen's, her voice flatter.

"I am not often asked," Lettice answered in her complaining way.

"Then we must make amends."

Elizabeth forced herself to speak warmly. "You are welcome."

It was not entirely true. On the few occasions that she had seen Lettice she had always begun by vowing to treat her as a friend and ended by wishing her elsewhere.

"I could not endure the country one moment longer," Lettice said. "Nothing ever happens there, save that the grass grows and my husband finds some new fault in me."

"Surely not!" Elizabeth forced into her memory the picture of the earl's long, fair face and mild blue eyes. "I thought your marriage a contented one."

"Oh, I am content enough," Lettice said. "Your Grace chose the better part by remaining single. Husbands and children are a constant source of anxiety."

"Are they indeed?" Elizabeth said.

"The estates do not yield as much as we had hoped," Lettice confided. "My lord was hoping to be given the governorship of Ireland to augment his income."

And had sent his wife to Court to plead poverty. The queen felt a heaviness of spirit fall upon her. If one of her blood relations were to tell her they needed nothing, craved only her company — she would give then with both hands and not count the cost.

"I will speak to Milord Burleigh," she said wearily. "He is godfather to your son, is he not?"

"To Robert, yes." Even in the fading light it was possible to see the softening of the other's rather hard features. "He is eight years old now and marvellously forward for his age. I am fortunate to have such a beautiful son."

"You must bring him to Court one day," Elizabeth said, making to pass.

"I would place him for rearing in some noble household and grant his host the wardship," Lettice said, "but I swear one doesn't know what to do for the best."

Wardships were leased for high fees. Lettice was uncertain which waters to fish in.

"I believe my lord of Leicester might agree to take the boy and see him educated as his rank demands," Elizabeth said.

It would serve Robin right to be saddled with the care of another small boy when he was refusing to acknowledge his own by Douglas Sheffield as legitimate. And Lord knows but he was rich enough. She had recently given him fifty thousand pounds as an outright gift, partly because she guessed his gambling debts to be unmanageable, partly because she wanted to make it crystal clear that her intended marriage to a prince of France in no way altered her regard for him.

"Ask Milord Leicester if he will accept the wardship," she advised. "You have my leave."

"Your Grace is always so generous," Lettice said neatly.

"Not always." Elizabeth gave her

cousin a frowning glance. "In future, when you come to our Court have the goodness to present yourself first to me."

"Of course, Your Grace. I but hesitated to trouble you." Lettice swept into a curtsy that had something mocking in its flourish.

"No trouble. You are welcome provided there are sufficient chambers."

"I brought only a few of my ladies with me," Lettice said, widening her brown eyes. "I do hope they will not inconvenience Your Grace."

"You must take care that they do not."

Weary of the game of cat and mouse, since she was beginning to wonder which animal was which, Elizabeth nodded curtly and continued on her way. Without glancing back she was aware of the other's hard scrutiny. Lettice, herself, looked much younger than her years. Her husband was said to be both loving and indulgent, and she had a family of young children, yet she carried about with her an air of discontent. The truth was that she had always resented the fact that while her mother had been only King Harry's mistress he had married Anne Boleyn. Lettice would dearly have loved to inherit a throne.

In the Council Chamber debate was already lively, several of her advisers being of the opinion that the eloping children of Lennox and Shrewsbury ought to be sent into the Tower along with their respective mothers. Rising and bowing as the queen entered they resumed their argument the instant she was seated, their voices vigorous and emphatic.

"It is no less than the Lady Katherine did when she matched herself without leave to Milord Hertford," Sussex was rumbling.

"Not to mention her sister who hurried to imitate the offence," Hatton put in.

Both the fair, frail sisters of Lady Jane had died imprisoned in the Tower for making marriages that threatened the stability of the succession. Elizabeth had not yet forgiven herself though she still could not see how she could have behaved differently.

"The case is altered now." She rapped sharply on the table to gain attention. "There were then factions who would have welcomed a descendant of Mary Rose Tudor upon the throne, but I have yet to hear one voice raised in favour of a Lennox — Shrewsbury rebellion. Our country is more stable, the people better contented, and my own forthcoming marriage will speedily reassure all men concerning the succession."

"Is Your Grace fully determined upon this alliance?" Arundel enquired.

"You all must realize by this time that I am most serious in my intention, if the prince be to our liking. They assure me that his complexion is much improved."

"Madam, it is not the complexion but your own constitution that troubles my heart," Sussex said bluntly. "You are forty years old, and at that age any woman, be she queen or commoner, must hesitate before she embarks for the first time upon matrimony."

"My physician tells me that I am most healthy and ripe for matrimony." Though she spoke calmly her face had flushed darkly.

"Your Grace ought to consider heredity too," the old earl insisted. "Your grandsire, it is true, fathered four living children but of those the Prince Arthur died at sixteen, and your own father though he took six wives could produce only three children from them of whom — "

"Her Grace surely knows her own family history without prompting," Heneage interposed. It was not an encouraging one. The Tudors were apt to produce sickly girls when they were able to produce living heirs at all. Her sister had been unable to conceive though at the end she believed that she had given birth to twins and died without realizing that the swelling in her belly was dropsy. Mary's thin, anxious face with the intense, fanatical dark eyes flashed into Elizabeth's mind.

"We cannot be constrained by old tales of woe," she said briskly. "You forget that both my sister and brother were delicate from birth whereas I was always a strong, forward babe. My governess used to sigh that she was sometimes tempted to wish some childish ailment upon me just to curb my mischievous high spirits."

"But Your Grace is not a child," Sussex said obstinately. "You are not a young woman any longer and a first child at your age must needs present a risk that I for one would be unwilling to countenance."

"It is not you who will be conceiving the child," she said crossly.

"But it is Your Grace who will bear it and in view of your age — "

"For God's sake, Milord Sussex, will you stop arguing on my age?" She banged her hand down on the table

214

more loudly. "Are you now become a doctor to inform us of medical matters? Go to! Ever since I came to the throne I have been urged to wed though for my own part I'd choose a maiden life, but you have all importuned me to take first this man and then the other as husband, and now that my mind is fixed upon France you sing a doleful song of warning as if I were already half in my dotage."

She broke off abruptly, staring down at her clenched fist, seeing through a mist of humiliating tears the faint tracery of raised blue veins showing more clearly through the white skin, seeing middle age like a spectre in the midst of the Council Chamber.

8

THE negotiations with France had dragged on into their second year with first one side and then another bringing up fresh objections. The prince must be granted the Crown Matrimonial but would not insist on practising his own Catholic faith. He wished to have new portraits of Her Grace for he feared she might have altered since he had first gazed upon her lineaments. The queen fretted lest the reported improvement in the prince's skin had been exaggerated and constantly mourned his lack of inches.

"It will be a great relief to enjoy ourselves at Kenilworth," Elizabeth said thankfully as the time for her visit to Leicester's estate grew near.

The earl had been absent from Court for months at a time and though she amused herself with the flirtations of Oxford, Hatton and Heneage, she missed her most constant and loving companion. This visit would mark the climax of her summer progress into Warwickshire, and set the seal on their long relationship.

"For Anjou must understand that my marriage with him cannot interfere with old friendships," Elizabeth said firmly. "Now if only the foolish boy would consent to travel here so that I might meet him personally my last little qualm might be stilled."

Anjou who had been Alencon, however, was detained in France, his mother declaring that her son could hardly be expected to present himself on approval. So, for the moment, the matter was shelved and the Court prepared for the visit.

"We shall ride to Kenilworth in hunting array," Elizabeth decided, wafting into the room where her maidservants were packing the garments she would wear. For the ten day sojourn she had signified her intention of taking thirty outfits with her, all of them ready made. With each gown went shoes, gloves, hats, jewels, sashes and cloaks, each item carefully labelled so that Her Grace could change at a moment's notice.

"Which dress will Your Grace wear?" Madge Scudamore looked questioning.

"The scarlet velvet," Elizabeth said, "with the gold plumed hat."

When she chose her wardrobe she was always brisk and swift, a fact joked about by her ladies who wondered why she could not make up her mind to marry with the same speed. They joked out of their royal mistress's hearing, however, since she was apt to become short tempered when the question of matrimony came up.

"That will look splendid," Kat Ashley said from her seat by the window.

There was nothing but enthusiasm in her face, but Elizabeth, with a quick glance, crossed to her side.

"What ails you, Ash Cat? Is it the

old pain again?" she asked gently.

"It grips me cruelly," Kat confessed.

"It would be better for you to rest here and not ride into Warwick?"

"If Your Grace craves my attendance then I will ride," Kat said. "Perhaps a litter? I am near seventy."

"Pooh, you think too much of your years," Elizabeth scolded. "You are scarce middle-aged."

"Then for your sake I hope to live to be an hundred and forty," Kat said with a wincing smile.

"You will dance at my wedding yet," Elizabeth said, "but I need you not in Warwick. I cannot flirt and giggle under your disapproving eye. You were always strict with me."

"I always spoiled you," Kat said. "You mind the night you went unchaperoned on the river with Sir Thomas Seymour? Ah, I ought to have prevented you that time for you put your reputation at risk, but you pleaded so piteously to be allowed to go, that I could not say nay. You were fourteen years old and like a green apple with the blossom still clinging to the stalk."

"Aye, we were all younger then," Elizabeth said. "Go and rest, Ash Cat. If you are not well again when I return from Warwick I shall be in a bad humour."

She patted the other on the shoulder and went out humming. In the passage the humming stopped and she stood, her hands clenched, fighting back terror. Burleigh, approaching and seeing her face, hesitated, wondering what new anxiety came to fret her.

"There you are." She took a long breath and went to meet him, shaking her head as he began to sink to his knees. "If you do that I may have to pick you up again. Your gout troubles you, I see."

"It is no more than age, Your Grace. I am past fifty," he said.

"How is it," Elizabeth said in sudden irritation, "that everybody is suddenly obsessed with age? Kat is sick again. It is the old pain that troubles her. She has been talking of the past, wandering through the landscape of my girlhood. What does that bode?"

"Your Grace has already divined it," he said gently.

"She has been with me since I was a child," Elizabeth said. "She knows all the secrets of my heart. Perhaps I ought to postpone the visit?"

"That would surely distress her greatly," Burleigh said.

"You are right. I must bid her au revoir with a smile and so, heigh-ho for Kenilworth."

A few days later she rode out on the first stage of her summer progress. Kat had waved from the window but Elizabeth, raising her riding-crop in salute, knew that she would not see her again, and felt a piercing grief. But Kat would have been the last person to want her to be sad. She turned her lips resolutely upwards and cantered on.

They came to the deer-park that surrounded Kenilworth early in July. There was a pleasure in the fact that

Leicester had invited her and she had not, as was her custom, first signified her intention of staying with him. She was conscious of and amused by the fact that not all her hosts were delighted when she informed them she would be coming to stay. The expense of entertaining the whole Court of almost a thousand persons had almost ruined many lords.

But Leicester was very rich. She had showered gifts and money on him during the seventeen years of her reign. Kenilworth itself had been a royal castle since the time of Edward the First. It had pleased her to bestow it on him, to accept his invitation. Ahead of her lay the inevitability of a political alliance but these days were for Robin and herself.

The honey-scented twilight of a July evening was shrouding the trees as the cavalcade rode up to the outer gate. Their coming had been well advertised. Out of the gloom light sparkled from a small lodge at the main gates and a burly porter stepped out to declaim a poem hailing the advent of a goddess. It would be the first of many eulogies to which she would listen during her stay. She wondered if Leicester had composed the halting verse, accepted the great key which the porter handed up to her and rode on, over the drawbridge to the inner bailey. Halfway across the drawbridge a veiled lady waited with flowers to bid her welcome in the name of the lady of the lake and hand up a bouquet.

Leicester had gone ahead to make final preparations for her coming. She looked eagerly about her as squires came to assist her from her mount.

He was there, tall, slightly too corpulent, but still her dearest Robin. She was rather less delighted to see the figure at his side, attired in blue damask.

"Milord Leicester invited me to be hostess to Your Grace," Lettice said, sinking into a deep curtsy, then bustling forward two tall children — "I think you have not met your second cousins — my son, Robert, and my daughter, Penelope. Robert is in ward to Milord Leicester."

Which was no reason for Lettice to preen herself as if she were mistress of the place. Her long-faced husband was campaigning in Ireland. Elizabeth wished his wife had accompanied him. Then her momentary displeasure was swept away as Leicester came to kiss her hand and lead her into the screened hall. As he did so every lamp in the dim castle was illumined, and his voice rang out.

"The coming of Her Grace wakes this castle into life again. Let every clock be stopped, for while Elizabeth of England is under my roof time itself shall stand still."

"Very pretty, upon my word," she approved, laughing. "You have become a poet, Robin."

"Alas, no." His dark eyes smiled at her. "I have spent my life in hopeless loving and my muse never came."

"Not hopeless surely?" she murmured, slanting a teasing glance.

At that moment it almost seemed possible that the clocks could be, not only stopped, but turned back to render them boy and girl again.

She was pleased that her cousin, Lettice, having played her part in the ceremony of welcome, sank into the background again. Elizabeth gave her credit for having the sense to know when it was useless to enter into competition. Her two children seemed charming, with the grace and good manners that their mother lacked. She saw them later, standing hand in hand, their faces raised to watch the display of fireworks which marked the end of supper.

The next day being Sunday the Court went to church, though the increased size of the regular congregation meant that many had to stand in the yard outside. Despite that there were many to cheer Elizabeth when she emerged, her scarlet riding dress changed for a green gown and little veiled hat which formed a perfect background for the sapphires she had chosen to wear.

"God save your sweet self from all enemies!" a stout matron exclaimed loudly as the queen passed her.

"God grant I have none here," Elizabeth answered smilingly, and let her gaze linger for an instant on her cousin, Lettice.

The other woman looked sour. No doubt she hated having her nose put out of joint. She had fondly imagined that she would continue to act the gracious hostess, giving no heed to the truth that wherever the queen came there could be no woman higher.

"May I escort Your Grace to your mount?"

Robert Devereux, Lettice's small son, had offered his arm with all the gravity of a full-grown courtier. He had waving auburn hair and bright, long-lashed grey eyes which had scarcely strayed from the queen except when the fireworks blazed.

"That is most kind of you, sir."

It was strange that the ungracious Lettice and her long-faced earl had between them managed to produce two younglings of consummate charm. Penelope, the girl, had lighter hair and darker eyes than her brother.

Smiling her thanks to the boy, Elizabeth, her mouth suddenly wistful, wondered if one day she would be able to look at a child of her own and marvel that between them she and Anjou had managed to produce such a paragon.

"What delights have you for the Sabbath, Robin?" she enquired of Leicester.

"Dancing in the garden this afternoon and fireworks tonight," he answered promptly.

"Then I will wear a pastoral dress. When I was a girl I often longed to be a milkmaid and wander in the meadows all day."

"I believe that real milkmaids do rather more than that."

"It was but a fantasy." She smiled at

him, thinking that it was no bad thing to live now and then in fantasy.

The days of fantasy continued. The weather was so warm that she spent the greater part of the mornings within doors but after midday she went hunting, watched the pageants that had been devised for her entertainment, danced and played upon the lute, flirted with Robin as if they also were younglings again.

If she could live thus for ever, she thought, she would be perfectly content. Yet there were moments when a queer restlessness overcame her and she found herself thinking for a spell of the intrigues and treacheries that were going on outside these enchanted walls.

Midway through the visit came word that Elizabeth Cavendish had borne Charles Darnley a daughter, Arbella.

"You may convey my congratulations and a silver christening cup," she informed Paget. "I am sure that I wish both mother and child well."

"What of the grandmothers?" Leicester

enquired, leaning on the arm of her chair.

"Lord, are they still in the Tower?" She put her hand to her mouth, laughing. "Well, their respective husbands have had a well earned break from scolding. I will send orders for their release."

"The babe is important in the succession, is she not?" Lettice said, in the innocently questioning bland tone that betokened spite.

"She is not in the least important," Elizabeth said coldly. "When my own marriage is finally celebrated then I shall provide heirs in plenty to render all those who preen themselves on being in the succession as supremely unimportant."

"I will pray for a safe delivery for Your Grace," Lettice said, outwardly meek.

The thought that it was dangerous to bear a first child when one was past forty knocked at her heart. She rose abruptly, saying with a little snap,

"This talk of babes is tedious, don't you think? I wish Arbella a long and happy life in the obscurity of Yorkshire. Robin, did you not say you had a bear-baiting planned?"

"With some splendid dogs matched against them," he agreed.

"In my grandfather's time there was once a bear-baiting when the dogs won," Elizabeth said, not looking at her cousin. "He ordered the dogs hanged for he deemed it not fitting that curs should overcome a nobler beast."

It was a good baiting, with fur flying and the smell of blood scenting the breeze with savagery. Watching, the queen felt something rise up in her that was very close to desire, and with the desire came the churning terror she had felt as a child when the gigantic figure of her father strode into view, accompanied by the smaller figure of her current stepmother.

On the last day there was a water pageant with maidens attired as nymphs floating on huge shells in the lake and the god Arion rising up through a cunningly concealed shaft to declaim yet another interminable poem of praise. This effort, however, ended rather more quickly than was anticipated. The man playing the role stumbled over a word, transposed a line, and in frustration tugged off his cumbersome headpiece, declaring loudly,

"I'm no Arion, not me, but honest Harry Goldingham as you may all plainly see."

"Your Grace, I will speak to the fellow," Leicester began in consternation, but she turned sparkling eyes on him, crying,

"Oh, give him a handsome reward, I pray you. His words were the best part of the performance."

On that final evening she eschewed the dancing and the tumbling of some acrobats who had been conveyed to the castle and elected instead to walk quietly through the grounds, a cloak over her shoulders, Leicester at her side.

"For these have truly been enchanted days, Robin," she said softly. "They have refreshed my spirit and made my year a happy one. I do thank you for inviting me to stay."

"I would have you remain," he said.

"Ah, it's a milkmaid dream," she said wistfully.

"It need not be. Bess, it need not be. Why cannot we be married? God knows I have been devoted to your person since we were children. Born in the same hour on the same day of the same year, remember? Our destinies march together."

"But not up the aisle," she said. "And you have had two wives."

"I was never legally joined to Douglas Sheffield."

"She believes that you were, and you have acknowledged her child as your own. If we married there would always be those to whisper about the legality of our union."

"First Amy's death and now Douglas Sheffield," he said wryly. "Obstacles arise which made it easy for you to hold me off. It has been thus with all your suitors."

"I cannot help the way fortunes fall," she said with a touch of sulkiness. "Why must you bring this old question up on my last evening here?"

"I was hoping this visit would be a prelude to something in which we both could rejoice."

"It is a climax, my dear. It is my way of telling the world that even if I wed a dozen French princes, you are the man who reigns supreme in my heart," she said softly.

"Is that truly your last word?" He swung her about to face him, his dark eyes boring into her paler ones, his fingers digging into the thin silk of her dress.

"Truly, Robin," she said sadly.

"Then I wish you joy and will be your most loving friend," he said, and the very absence of any caress told her how deeply he was moved. "I have hoped against hope for too long. There must come an ending of such dreaming that never can come true. One thing you must believe. I do not love the crown you wear or the throne you sit on. I love Elizabeth the woman and will go on loving her to the end of my life."

"As I love you," she said, and thought suddenly that all this was but part of the masque in which they both performed, saying their set pieces, dancing the measure that had been set to music before they were both born.

They walked on in silent unity while the moon rose higher and within the great hall her courtiers applauded the skill of the hired acrobat.

The next morning she left Kenilworth, clad in the scarlet habit she had worn on her arrival, hearing Leicester's order,

"Start the clocks again."

At the gate her cousin Lettice swept her a deep curtsy, holding her two children by the hands.

Elizabeth looked down at her, a faint frown creasing her brows. "Have you no home of your own, cousin?" she asked.

"A lonely one, Your Grace, since my husband is detained still in Ireland."

Such a meek voice from the thin scarlet mouth.

"You must return there and sweeten the house against his coming," Elizabeth said. Lettice infinitely preferred giving herself airs as hostess at Kenilworth to acting the chatelaine on her own lord's estates. If looks could slay, Elizabeth reflected, then she herself would now be lying dead under the hooves of her mount.

Kat Ashley had died during her absence. Somewhere in the back of her mind Elizabeth had known it would be so, but it was a link of love snapped all the same. Kat Ashley had Boleyn blood and had known Anne Boleyn well, had guarded her child though not always acted wisely in the matter of the romance Elizabeth had had with Sir Thomas Seymour; she had always been there, first as governess and then as companion. The number of those with whom the queen could be entirely herself, speaking her mind without fear of misrepresentation, was few, and now was diminished by one.

She buried herself in work, keeping her councillors on the run often until after midnight as she demanded fresh information, wrote another letter, argued yet again against bringing the Queen of Scots to trial. In protecting Mary Stuart she was protecting her own dignity, she felt, for when one queen is brought low another may be pulled down later.

"If only Anjou would consent to pay a visit so that I could take a good look at him," she grumbled, "I would be happier about this proposed marriage. I myself have no fear about being seen, so what holds him back?"

"Queen Catherine's latest suggestion is that Your Grace should travel to France," Burleigh said.

"So the French could hold me hostage and marry Anjou to the Queen of Scots once they had released her and placed her upon our throne, of course," Elizabeth said wryly. "The Medici woman must fancy I am next door to an idiot and my Council are worse."

But she dictated a honeyed letter back, praising Queen Catherine for her wisdom and regretting that the rough seas that flowed between the two countries made such a suggestion one that her faint female spirit hesitated to cross.

"Faint female spirit is excellent, Madam." Her private secretary, Master Davison, looked up with a grin.

"It is neat," she admitted, and gave him an approving look. "I shall never leave England, you know. I was not destined to make long journeys."

Shorter journeys were a different matter. When she was not closeted in Council she was on the move, visiting Greenwich where her ships came and went with cargoes from an increasing number of lands, spending three days at Sandwich where she watched young Huguenot weavers working on the looms that were their livelihood, and informed the Catholic Courts of Europe that in England Protestants might find refuge.

"It is a fair country," she informed La Motte as they rode together in the park at Hatfield the following spring. "I would not change it for any other."

"Surely all monarchs must feel like that," the ambassador said.

"Not my cousin of Scots," Elizabeth said scornfully. "She has never hidden her contempt for Scotland nor her belief that England is the land she craves. Were I ruler of the most modest island in the world I would cherish every foot of my domain and let my people know it."

"And your people honour that in Your Grace's nature," he said.

"Of course. They recognize that I am mere English like themselves," she said serenely.

He hid a smile, thinking of the

mingled French, Spanish, Welsh and Norman blood that ran through her veins. Even her appearance was not English. The narrow face with the long sea-coloured eyes, the graceful Italianate hands, the crown of red gold hair which either through art or good fortune showed no threads of grey, were exotic, otherworldly, just as her stiff and spangled skirts, held wide over a farthingale, the huge ruffs that were like the sepals of a flower, and the plumed hats with their long gauzy veils were the garments of a woman who never needed to lift one finger on her own behalf.

"Oxford's wife is complaining again," she said, changing the subject. "You know he wed Milord Burleigh's daughter? A very good match for Ann Cecil is intelligent and loyal, but the foolish boy imagines himself in love with me and neglects her shamefully. I scold him about it."

"These foolishnesses will melt like snow in summer when the prince comes," La Motte said.

"Oh, do you think so?" She looked amused.

"Monsieur Simier has asked for leave to come to plead his master's suit," La Motte said. "I hope Your Grace will give him leave."

"Since Anjou will not plead his suit in person there is no other course. These delays are most fatiguing."

"Madam, you know well that were you to give a definite answer the Duke of Anjou would be here at your side within a few days," he said.

"And I cannot possibly give such an answer until I have seen him," she said. "Monsieur Simier will be a poor substitute, I fear. And I cannot agree to his coming until the mourning for the Earl of Essex is concluded. You know my poor cousin Lettice is widowed now? Her husband died in Ireland which is a great grief to us all. But when the mourning is over why then Monsieur Simier may prepare to set sail."

9

"I CANNOT believe it," Elizabeth said with decision, shaking her head. "It is all very well for you all to urge me to it, but it is not your tooth."

She was not looking her best on this bright May morning. Her cheek was distended and her eyes heavy from lack of sleep. Despite the poppy syrup that she had taken and the fenugreek that had been packed into the space between gum and tooth the pain had raged unabated.

"There was a waxen image of Your Grace found last week in the house of a priest at Islington," Sir Nicholas Bacon said gloomily. "I fear witchcraft."

"I hope the image was melted down," Paget said.

"Melted down and the priest imprisoned. There are too many of

241

these Jesuits creeping into the country. The recusancy laws ought to be tightened up."

"Which will not help Her Grace's toothache," Burleigh said.

"The chiropractor is ready to draw it," Hatton said.

"At the cost of some little pain," Leicester added encouragingly.

("It is but a little pain," the Lord Lieutenant had said to Anne Boleyn, and she, laughing, had put her hands to her throat, crying merrily,

"That's good, for I have but a little neck.")

"Nobody shall cut into my mouth," Elizabeth said wincingly.

"The tooth would be out in a moment," Burleigh declared.

"You are very quick," she said sourly, "to recommend surgery to me. I would like to know how your opinions would stand if it were your tooth that needed drawing."

"Your Grace." It was the elderly Bishop of London who spoke. "I haven't many teeth left, but I am most willing to lose one in your service."

"Call in the man. Let us see his art then," Burleigh said quickly, before the bishop could withdraw his offer.

The Council watched with interest as the chiropractor, bowing deeply, was admitted and proceeded to lay out his instruments. They looked, thought the queen shrinkingly, very sharp.

"The bishop wishes you to draw one of his teeth first," Leicester informed him. "By way of example."

"A back tooth," the bishop said.

"If Your Lordship will sit in this chair then near to the window?"

"How do you usually proceed?" Bacon enquired as the bishop obeyed.

"If the tooth has been loosened by fenugreek," the chiropractor said, "then it is a simple and speedy matter. Should the tooth be firmly rooted or the patient struggle then a tap upon the head generally suffices to quiet them long enough to extract the tooth."

"Good God! You cannot go knocking

Her Grace or the Bishop of London over the head," Hatton said in alarm.

"Such a proceeding will not be necessary," the bishop said with dignity.

"Allow me to look into your mouth, my lord bishop." The chiropractor had seized a large pair of pliers and bent down.

There was an instant's silence, a muffled yelp, and the chiropractor straightened up, a small white object stained with red gripped in the pliers.

"Was that it?" the bishop asked, opening his eyes.

"How do you feel?" Elizabeth said anxiously.

"A touch of soreness," Aylmer probed cautiously with the tip of his tongue.

"Your Grace?" It was Burleigh who spoke but they were all looking at her. She drew a quivering breath, and moved on shaking legs to the chair.

His shadow falling over her, the shock of cold steel, a wrenching pain and her own tooth was triumphantly held aloft. The Council applauded.

"It was but a little pain," Elizabeth said modestly, spitting blood into a basin that the chiropractor thrust under her nose.

"If Your Grace will rinse out your mouth with warm water and then take a drink of poppy juice the swelling will rapidly subside," he advised.

"And you shall be well rewarded for your skills," she said gratefully. "I shall rest for a day to recover from the operation."

"I would suggest two days," Leicester said. "It is no small thing to draw an abscessed tooth."

"Since when did you become a medical man?" Elizabeth demanded. "Tomorrow I am going to have private conference with Monsieur Simier and will not postpone it."

As she left the Council Chamber she was aware of the muttering that had broken out behind her.

It was now over a year since the small, dark diplomat had arrived, to persuade her to agree officially to a marriage with the Duke of Anjou. During that year he had established himself in her affections as an amusing and quick-witted courtier who courted her by proxy with great skill. Her Council were rather less enthusiastic, regarding him as a sneaking foreigner who mocked English customs behind everybody's backs.

Be that as it may Monsieur Simier had a genius for doing the imaginative thing, entering her presence on the following day with a gift that made her first stare and then laugh.

"A whale's tooth, set in gold? For heaven's sake, Monsieur, where did you find such a curiosity?"

"That is my secret, Your Grace. Perhaps I caught the great beast myself."

"Had it been a minnow's tooth," she said, "I might have believed you. Drake brings me similar curios from time to time."

She sighed briefly as she spoke, remembering that the sea captain was now on the high seas, determined to sail round the world.

"For I am sure it is round, Your Grace, and there are lands still undiscovered where we might plant the English flag and trade in safety."

"Or you might fall off the edge," she had retorted. "Well, if you must seek adventure then go, and if you ever return you will have hearty welcome."

"I hope that sigh was for my master," Simier said. "I swear to you that he sends forth a hundred sighs a day for the longing to be matched with Your Grace."

"As do I." She prepared to engage in the usual game of diplomatic insincerity.

"Your Grace, may I be frank?" His narrow face was serious for once, so serious that she gave him a surprised look.

"Is something wrong?" she asked sharply.

"Madam, what is wrong can be swiftly remedied by yourself," he said.

"This year you will be celebrating twenty years upon the throne. Twenty years during which you have played first with one suitor and then with another."

"That fault, if it be a fault, cannot be laid entirely at my door," she protested. "There have been circumstances that have often compelled me to hesitate."

"In September Your Grace will also celebrate your forty-fifth birthday," he said.

"How ungallant of you to remind me!"

"If Your Grace looked within ten years of that age then you might accuse me of ungallantry. As it is you pass without effort for a lady many years younger, as my master though he is only twenty-three in calendar years is actually far older in habits of mind and wisdom. But one cannot deny the clock."

"At Kenilworth we did," she said softly.

"And there's the rub! There is the

impediment," he exclaimed.

"Kenilworth?" She raised her plucked brows.

"Its master and there are those who say he is master also of the queen herself, that so strong is the love liking between you both that you never seriously consider any other husband, believing in some corner of your mind that one day it might yet be possible for Your Grace and Milord Leicester to wed."

"You are indeed being very frank," she said frowningly.

"Then let me be more frank yet. Your Grace, the Earl of Leicester has deceived you. He may love you for what man, having once seen you, could not? But he does not love you with that unswerving constancy that you deserve."

"If you are going to speak of Douglas Sheffield," she said wearily, "you may spare your breath. He has steadfastly maintained that it was no legal marriage. He has never lived with her nor acknowledged her boy as legitimate, and she is now declaring to anyone who will pay heed to her nonsense that he actually tried to poison her."

"I know nothing of that," Simier said, "but I was not speaking of Lady Sheffield. I speak of his existing marriage."

"Are you suffering from spring madness? Amy Robsart died long ago."

"Your Grace, Milord Leicester has been secretly wed these two years," Simier said.

"What?" Elizabeth stared at him, her eyes paling to ice. "That is a most foul slander."

"No slander, Your Grace. Milord Leicester was privately and legally married at his manor of Wanstead two years since."

"To whom?" she asked blankly.

"To Lettice, Countess of Essex," Simier said.

"You lie." Her voice was suddenly

250

dull. Only her eyes glittered. "My cousin, Lettice, was widowed two years ago and has since lived in strict retirement."

"There is a child," Simier said. "A boy whom Leicester has had baptised as his legitimate son."

"Robin is married?" She seemed to ask the question of the air behind him for her gaze cancelled out the presence of the diplomat. "He married Lettice?"

"My information has been checked and double checked," he said. "There are those of your Court who have suspected how matters stood, but being devoted to Your Grace, have said nothing. I too am devoted to your service and eager for your happiness which I believe you will find in the arms of my royal — "

"How you run on!" she said wonderingly. "So many words strung together down the years to weave a pattern in which I am trapped. Married to my cousin. How galling it must have been for Lettice not to be able to flaunt her triumph in my face."

"Madam?" he began, but she had risen and was striding from the room, her voice raised.

"Leicester! Leicester, where the devil are you? Leicester!"

"Here, Your Grace, at your command as ever." He came smilingly from an ante chamber, his lute in his hand.

"Where is your wife?" she demanded. "On whom does she dance attendance?"

"Douglas is not — "

"Oh, cease the pretending! I am not speaking of Douglas or of poor dead Amy. I refer to your present wife, to my cousin, Lettice Knollys who was the Countess of Essex until her husband died and she decided to be Countess of Leicester instead. Two years wed and nobody had the courage to tell me until now. Two years wed with a child and you stand there and dare to tell me you are at my command."

He had begun to bluster, his dark face crimsoning, but she rushed past him, flailing the air with her clenched fists, her voice rising to a shriek that brought her guards running with their weapons half drawn.

"Arrest the Earl of Leicester! Escort him to the Miraflore Tower and summon those of my Council who are within the palace. Why do you stand and gape at me?"

"To arrest the Earl of Leicester?" one of the guards repeated in astonishment.

"That is my order. Are you too traitors to disobey?"

"Bess, you're making a fool of yourself," Leicester said.

Swinging round she struck him resoundingly across the face, her eyes glinting in her white face.

"No woman," he said through his teeth, "ever raised a hand to me."

"One more word and I'll have your head! Guards! Milord Burleigh, why do you delay when you hear me calling for you?"

She rustled towards the sundry alarmed members of her Council who were appearing from several directions at once.

"Your Grace, what in God's Name has happened?" Burleigh cried, limping forward. "Why is Milord of Leicester in custody?"

"Because he is a foul traitor, keeping me from marriage and motherhood under the guise of loving devotion when these two years he has been the husband of that bitch, Lettice!"

She had entered the Council Chamber where she raged up and down, words spilling from her while, at each turn, she banged the long table, seeming unaware of the pain to her knuckles.

"Your Grace must be calm, I beg you," Burleigh said, raising his own voice. "There may be some explanation."

"Did you know of this?" She stopped pacing and faced him accusingly.

"I had heard rumours," he said unwillingly. "I discounted them as slanders put about by those who are jealous of the earl's great credit of many

254

years with Your Grace."

"You heard rumours," she mocked savagely. "No doubt you all heard rumours. Did none of you check those 'rumours'? Did none of you have the courage to tell me of such suspicions? You are all false traitors! It is not your will that I should be happy. God forbid that Elizabeth Tudor should enjoy the simple joys that even the humblest subject in the land has a right to claim! I will have Leicester's head for this. Aye, and hers too!"

"Your Grace's anger is justified," Burleigh said hastily, "but to act without due thought will worsen the matter. We must act within the law."

"What are you babbling about now, Cecil?" She flung herself, panting, into her chair, her bruised hand cupping her still swollen cheek.

"Your Grace's anger at the undutiful conduct of the earl is shared by all of us," Burleigh said temperately. "Like your royal self I am disgusted at this revelation, disgusted also at my own simplicity for I took the rumour as mere rumour and made no enquiry. However we are all bound by the rule of law, and must conduct ourselves accordingly."

"He shall be put on trial," she broke in.

"But on what charge, Your Grace?" Burleigh spread his hands wide. "What legal offences has he committed? Sir Christopher, you are the lawyer among us? What law has he broken?"

"Every law of devotion and courtesy," Hatton answered promptly, "but of other wrong-doing, such as is written in the Statute Book, none, I regret to say."

"Expound it to us," Burleigh invited.

"Milord Leicester is of mature years, considered in his right mind, of independent means, a widower of long standing. There is nothing to prevent him from marrying where he pleases."

"Without my permission? But I am his monarch," Elizabeth said, bewildered.

"He is a subject of Your Grace, and a most ungrateful one," Hatton told her, "but he has broken no law."

"He married Douglas Sheffield!"

"That was only an empty ceremony designed to placate the lady in question. It has no validity in law. He has broken no law within the strict meaning of the word."

"I would have him in the Tower to await my pleasure," she said harshly.

"Indeed he deserves it," Sussex interposed. "Damned gypsy fellow. Never trusted a Dudley!"

Something that might have been a guffaw escaped Burleigh. He hastily composed his face again and said,

"I am of the same opinion as Your Grace for he has offended most grievously, but we are constrained not only by law — indeed Your Grace indicated her displeasure at the Lennox marriage by sending both the respective mothers for a sojourn in the Tower — but if Your Grace takes similar action in this case there will be people to exclaim, most unfairly, that Your Grace acts thus not because there is any question of the succession being called into question, but out of female jealousy and spite."

"Are you suggesting that I am jealous of that whey-faced bitch?" Elizabeth asked, very low.

"Your Grace's nature is too noble to harbour such base considerations," he replied smoothly.

"Is it?" She looked at him doubtfully, worrying her thumbnail with her teeth.

"I can swear," he said earnestly, "that Your Grace's displeasure arises solely from the sheer effrontery and ingratitude of the pair. You have showered wealth and honours upon this man, and he has not even the good manners to inform you of his marriage nor of his child. Boy or girl?"

"A boy," she said.

"God grant that Your Grace may soon celebrate a similar happy event! Indeed, it is my belief that this sad affair may yet work to your advantage since now your eyes have been opened as to the duplicity of his protestations of undying faithfulness you will realize that you cannot be matched with any lower than a prince."

"Of Anjou, I suppose?"

"I believe that the young man waits anxiously for a kindly word regarding his suit."

"Perhaps we will consider the matter more deeply," she said slowly. "As for Leicester — "

"A mere parvenu, Your Grace, with no drop of royal blood, raised from comparative obscurity to be one of the noblest in the land. Of what interest is the marriage of such a one to you?"

"My father," she said viciously, "would have cut off his head."

"Yes, well — Your Grace's late lamented father did many things which today would not be countenanced by your own good sense," he answered.

"He is banished from Court," she said. "That, at least, lies still within my power."

"Madam, if you allow that blackguard anywhere near the Court," Sussex said, "I will resign my seat upon the Council."

"I never want to see him again." There was a pitiful bleakness in her face. "He swore lifelong fidelity to me, and I have forgiven him time after time. Time after time, gentlemen. Out of our long companionship — "

"And Your Grace's own noble and generous disposition," Hatton added.

"My generosity has been ill repaid," she said tightly. "I hope there are no others of my Court who have deceived me. You, Hatton, who swear you are still bachelor for love of me, do you have a wife tucked away somewhere?"

"God forbid, Your Grace!" he said in horror.

"Order him to Wanstead, and bid him stay there," she said, rage yielding to decision. "It is over between us for I have been most grossly deceived. I will never look upon his face again."

She waved her hand in dismissal,

nodding her head as they bowed and backed out. Hatton, the last to leave, gently closed the door behind him.

The empty room, the long table with its carved chairs, the windows through which the spring sunshine poured, all mocked her loneliness. Her missing tooth ached as if it were still in its socket and that morning she had plucked seven grey hairs from her head.

She dropped her head in her hands, feeling the hot tears run down her face, wanting Kat Ashley, wanting Tom Seymour, wanting to turn back time, whispering as she silently wept,

"'Tis only my tooth that pains me. Only that. Nothing more."

10

THE year had galloped past, leaving her breathless and dismayed in its wake. In a few months she would be forty-nine years old, that multiple of seven considered of particular importance by astrologers since it marked the little climacteric when a person might regard themselves as old. Which in her case was all nonsense, she told herself, because her courses still came every month though they had never been heavy nor lasted long. There were more lines in her face now though she painted skilfully enough to deceive, using the white powder that gave her complexion the translucent gleam of a pearl, and her hair was brightened with henna to a shade more vivid than when she had been a girl. Her figure was still slender and the new farthingales with the frame extending only to hip level left the overskirt to drop straight from its edge to the floor after the manner of a table-cloth, thus emphazising the height of the wearer. The long, pointed bodice thrust the skirt down at the front, tilting it slightly at the back and sleeves were huge and puffed, also supported by frames of whalebone. The closed ruff had been superseded by an open one that bared the throat and stood up behind like a fan, its edge frilled with lace. Hats were tiny, perched on short, curling hair, with brooches and feather plumes to hold up the brim. In such garments one must, of necessity, hold oneself straight and move with slow dignity.

In spring old hurts bubbled below the surface. She was restless and slept little, often waking with tears on her cheeks and no memory of dreaming.

"I do wish something exciting and miraculous would happen," she exclaimed to her ladies as they sat after supper one light, warm evening at Greenwich.

"So do I," Kate Carey said feelingly.

The queen sent her a look in which exasperation and affection were mingled. She was fond of the daughters of William Carey, the son whom Mary Boleyn had borne officially to her legal husband though it was freely rumoured that William had been the son of old Harry the Eighth. That made them doubly her nieces, she reflected, and wished that their aunt on the maternal side were not the abominable Lettice whose name she could not bring herself to pronounce. But both Kate and Philadelphia were lively and lovely girls, making her laugh with their quick enthusiasm, their whole-hearted adoration of herself.

"Let us make a wish." Philadelphia threw down the piece of silk she was embroidering and closed her eyes tightly.

"You ought to wish on something," Kate said severely. "On a wishbone or a hare's foot."

"There is chicken on the table in

the other room," Kate said, opening her eyes and jumping up.

"Ring for a servant," Elizabeth began chidingly, but the girl had already whisked out.

"She is a dreadful romp, Your Grace," Philadelphia disapproved, looking after her.

"Let her alone. She makes me laugh," Elizabeth said indulgently.

"Oh, Your Grace!" From the inner room Kate's voice rose into a squeal.

"What ails the silly girl now?" Elizabeth began, and broke off in mid-air as a young man, wrapped in a dark, travel-grimed cloak, burst in and swept off his feathered hat, crying in French.

"Your Grace, I come!"

"Coming or going, who are you?" she demanded sharply.

"Shall I summon the guard?" Mary Scudamore whispered nervously.

"Not until I have looked my fill at that sweet face," the stranger declared. "Oh, Madam, you are so much above your portrait as the sun is above the moon. Am I better or worse than mine?"

"Than your — ?" Elizabeth broke off, peering more closely at the pockmarked skin, the large nose set between sparkling black eyes. "Is it possible?" she said slowly.

"Not possible, but certain, Madame." The black eyes danced. "I, Francis of Anjou, am here."

"Good God!" Elizabeth said blankly. "How the devil did you get in?"

"I climbed over the back wall and bribed a cook in the scullery to let me up the back stairs," the French prince said cheerfully. "I am here incognito, Your Grace. I crossed the Channel in disguise with only two companions to implore you either to kill me or to agree to marry me. These negotiations have dragged on too long. We together will assert the triumph of love over expediency."

"You are actually here." She was still staring at him, but the corners of her mouth were twitching. "Who knows of this?"

"Not even my lady mother," he assured her. "That is why I dare not stay more than a day or two, long enough for you to fall in love with me — for you will, you know, for all that I am little and ugly. For my own part I am already in love with you, and I shall only fall more deeply in love with every moment I remain in your company. Now do bid me welcome and tell me that I have cause to hope or give me leave to kill myself instantly."

"Would you really kill yourself?" she enquired.

His smile was dazzling. "Alas, Your Grace, I have always been a miserable coward," he said. "But I would spend the rest of my life in the most abject misery."

The queen stared at him for a moment later and then threw back her curled head and began to laugh — hearty, side-holding mirth that brought tears to her eyes and a flush to her cheeks that owed nothing to art.

"We were just now wishing for excitement," she said, wiping her eyes weakly. "You have provided it in overflowing measure. My Lord of Anjou, you are most heartily welcome."

"Will you not honour me by calling me as your betrothed husband with my Christian name?" he begged.

"You run too fast for me, sir," she said. "I am a maiden lady that cannot be bustled into love liking like a peasant."

"To hear my name on your lips — that will be a supreme pleasure when you grant it to me," he said wistfully.

"First we must find you lodging, and then send word to your relatives that you are not dead or stolen away by pirates," she said. "To come here, like lightning on a summer day, and cozen me with your nonsense. This is madness indeed."

But she was laughing again as she

spoke, her eyes shining as she led him from the room.

"Mad," Burleigh said the next morning, having hurried to the palace upon receiving the intelligence of the prince's arrival. "Quite mad. What possessed His Highness to act with such contempt for custom and etiquette?"

"He wished to see me face to face," Elizabeth said, "and he tells me that he likes what he sees so well that he wishes to marry me tomorrow."

"Your Grace was not thinking — ?"

"Of course not. The agreement must be drawn up and signed and ratified, but I tell you that I like him well. He is much more attractive than I was ever led to believe."

"He is very short," Hatton said from his stance by the window.

"Are characters now measured in inches?" she asked irritably. "His figure is graceful and well proportioned and he has a most charming voice."

"And he is pockmarked," Hatton persisted.

"Your jealousy is showing, Sir Christopher," she said, looking pleased. "You knew that I have always intended to marry him."

"Your Grace also considered wedding both his older brothers first," Hatton muttered.

"I find him much more attractive than I imagined," she said, ignoring the remark. "I was not shown a portrait that did him justice. Indeed no portrait can do him justice, for I understand now that it is in his grace, his smile and the cadences of his voice that his beauty lies, and no brush can express those qualities adequately."

"His conduct verges on the reckless," Burleigh said, shaking his grey head. "If the vessel in which he sailed had been sunk or taken by pirates, I shudder to think of the repercussions to Anglo-French relations."

"He is a young man in love," Elizabeth said. "He tells me that I too am far lovelier than any portrait he has seen."

At that moment it was true. Her face was softer and rounder than he had seen it, with a sparkle in her eyes and a happy smile playing about her lips. She was wearing a green dress embroidered all over with golden butterflies and a frog brooch pinned her tiny velvet cap to her head.

"I have sent despatches to the King and Queen Mother of France, reassuring them that the duke is safe and will be returning to his own land in a day or two," Burleigh said. "As he came incognito perhaps he can be induced to leave in the same manner."

"And the marriage negotiations will be speeded up?" Her voice was eager.

"Madam, you yourself were the one who wished to delay," he said reproachfully. "Now you chide us for procrastination."

"Well, see to it," she said mildly.

She was all mildness for the next week, her voice gentle, her laughter frequently ringing out. And the Duke of Anjou was constantly at her side, his head. barely reaching her shoulder, his nose 'leading the rest of him', as Kate Carey whispered out of earshot of the queen. The queen herself seemed sublimely indifferent to the difference in their heights or their ages. Anjou made criticism useless because he was the first to poke fun at his own inadequacies.

"Do you know the name first bestowed upon me at my christening?" he asked her as they sat together on the afternoon of his departure.

She shook her head.

"Hercules," he informed her. "Can you imagine a less suitable name for me? When my eldest brother died it was decided to bequeath his name of Francis to me, and though I grieved for him I was glad of his name."

"You must have been a forward child to grieve," Elizabeth said. "You were only a baby."

"Oh, I was always an elderly baby," he said solemnly. "It was almost decided to make me an archbishop when I was six, but I was so small it would have been difficult for me to see over the top of the pulpit."

She burst out laughing at the picture he conjured up and then abruptly sobered.

"When you were six," she said, "I was already past thirty and sat upon the throne."

"You are going to tell me that I am only a boy," he said, taking her hand and kissing each finger separately. "Dearest and most potent queen, you must not mistake my jesting for levity of heart. In matters of love I have known for a long time that I would be content only with the most beautiful woman in the world and I have known in my heart that I would find her here. The difference in our ages makes no matter. I love you sufficiently for two of my age, so I am equal to anyone of forty-six."

"You have sufficient charm for ten," she said, laughing again. "Upon my word, Anjou, what am I to do with you?"

"Invite me to return to these shores officially and sign the marriage articles," he said promptly.

"I will do it." She spoke with decision. "Will you come back, Francis?"

"With more pleasure than lips can tell," he said, and reaching up from the stool where he sat, took her face between his hands and kissed her full on the mouth.

"And so it goes," said Burleigh, turning from his vantage point. "Her Grace is run clean mad for love of this French prince. She does not see his lack of dignity, his rash conduct, or his ugliness. She has forgotten that in the prevailing climate a Catholic marriage will be less than popular. Thank the Lord he sails on the evening tide else he might persuade her to put her pride in her pocket and elope with him."

"She is infatuated," his companion said.

"More than I could have believed

possible," Burleigh agreed. "Hatton and Heneage and the rest are nowhere, since they speak honest English and are not pockmarked."

"Did not Sir Philip Sidney remonstrate with her?"

"And was packed off to his country estate for his pains. One, John Stubbs, has published a broadsheet, advising the queen to think well before she takes a husband so much younger than herself. The fellow is right, though he has been arrested for sedition."

"And rightly so," the other growled. "In this age every man thinks he can speak out on any subject he pleases whether he be knight or villain."

Burleigh, like his companion, modestly descended, nodded agreement as they moved away.

The ship that was to carry the impulsive Anjou back to France was berthed at the dock. Elizabeth would have gone on board with him to say her farewell, but Sussex pointed out that as the prince had come incognito such behaviour would cause a scandal.

"To which opinion I must bow. There was never any woman less free to please herself than I," she sighed.

"When I return it will be with trumpets blaring and the wedding ring in my pocket," he promised.

"Come soon."

They stood in the garden, himself dressed for travelling, the groom holding the horse that would bear him to the water's edge.

"Very soon," he said, and mounted up, leaning to lay his hand along her cheek. "Madam, I came in a spirit of defiance, tired of delays and obstructions, half believing that you were merely playing with me. I leave reassured and comforted on all matters and completely in love with Your Grace's sweet person. When next I come it will be to claim you as my wife."

Then he was galloping away, turning once to doff his plumed hat.

The garden was chilly though the

sun had not gone in. She shivered without knowing why, blinking tears from her eyes and seeing, as she raised her head, the tall figure of the man who had accompanied Burleigh earlier in the day.

"Rob — Milord of Leicester, who gave you leave to approach my Court?" she demanded, her brows rushing together in a frown.

"I broke bounds," he said, "in order to have one glimpse of the lady who holds my heart. Now you may consign me to the Tower if you choose."

"I do not see Cousin Lettice anywhere," she said.

"It is not Lettice who holds my heart. Don't you know that I only wed her because — ?"

"Because she reminded you of me," Elizabeth finished. "Oh, Robin, when will you cease treating me like a fool? That excuse you used up with Douglas Sheffield."

"You know me too well," he said ruefully.

"And trust you not at all." She had moved nearer, her hand reaching to pat his sleeve. "We are too much alike, you and I. We have always played the same game."

"Making up our own rules," he said. "If I am forced to stay longer at Wanstead counting sheep I shall run crazy."

"I am going to marry Anjou," she said. "That is no game."

"Do you love him?"

"As much as you love my cousin Lettice."

"Then I need not be jealous," he said, smiling slightly.

"Your boy by her died, did he not?" Her tone had gentled. "I was sorry to hear it."

"Aye, he was a noble imp." Sorrow had rushed into his face.

"You have gained overmuch weight," she said sharply, "and your hair is greying."

"Also thinning," he said wryly.

"I will give you a lotion to help that.

My own hair is still thick and as red as when I was twenty."

"Redder," he said.

"Impudent." She aimed a blow at him but he caught both her hands, looking down at her.

"You really mean to wed Anjou?" he said.

"I really do," she answered him. "I am in love, Rob. I had thought it could never happen to me again. You love Lettice, don't you?"

"Yes," he said simply.

"And those other loves cannot spoil what we two share?"

"Nothing could spoil that, my Bess," he said.

She was silent for a space, her eyes remembering, and then she laughed. "Kiss me then, Robin," she invited. "Let us make a small scandal in the Court."

"Not for that reason but for love," Leicester said, and kissed her heartily, as if they were boy and girl again.

WITH SOMEBODY ELSE
Theresa Charles

Rosamond sets off for Cornwall with Hugo to meet his family, blissfully unaware of the shocks in store for her.

A SUMMER FOR STRANGERS
Claire Hamilton

Because she had lost her job, her flat and she had no money, Tabitha agreed to pose as Adam's future wife although she believed the scheme to be deceitful and cruel.

VILLA OF SINGING WATER
Angela Petron

The disquieting incidents that occurred at the Vatican and the Colosseum did not trouble Jan at first, but then they became increasingly unpleasant and alarming.

DOCTOR NAPIER'S NURSE
Pauline Ash

When cousins Midge and Derry are entered as probationer nurses on the same day but at different hospitals they agree to exchange identities.

A GIRL LIKE JULIE
Louise Ellis

Caroline absolutely adored Hugh Barrington, but then Julie Crane came into their lives. Julie was the kind of girl who attracts men without even trying.

COUNTRY DOCTOR
Paula Lindsay

When Evan Richmond bought a practice in a remote country village he did not realise that a casual encounter would lead to the loss of his heart.